# The Storm Of Shadows

Kirsten Yates

Published by Kirsten Yates, 2024.

This is a work of fiction. Similarities to real people, places, or events are entirely coincidental.

THE STORM OF SHADOWS

**First edition. November 18, 2024.**

Copyright © 2024 Kirsten Yates.

ISBN: 979-8230244165

Written by Kirsten Yates.

# Chapter 1

The wind howled through the narrow streets of the village, carrying with it an eerie chill that made even the bravest soul's shiver. Dark clouds swirled ominously in the sky, casting unnatural shadows across the land. The *Storm of Shadows* had arrived.

Elias stood at the edge of the village, his hood pulled low over his face, watching as the storm slowly encroached. He had been tracking it for days, following its destructive path through desolate towns and empty cities. Every step had brought him closer to something he did not fully understand, but he knew one thing for certain—the storm was not natural.

The wind seemed to whisper to him, carrying voices that he could not shake. Words he could not quite understand. At first, he thought it was his imagination playing tricks on him, but the whispers had grown louder with each passing day. Now, standing at the edge of this dying village, they were almost deafening.

"*The shadows are coming. The shadows will consume.*"

The words echoed in his mind, sending a shiver down his spine. He tightened his grip on the hilt of the sword strapped to his back, as if the cold steel could somehow protect him from the voices.

Around him, villagers hurried to close their doors and shutter their windows. No one wanted to be outside when the storm hit. Rumors had spread like wildfire in the taverns and marketplaces: entire towns wiped off the map, people disappearing without a trace, and those who survived claiming to have seen dark, shadowy figures moving within the storm.

Elias had seen them too.

The first time had been three nights ago, in the ruins of an old castle at the edge of the storm. He had been searching for shelter when he caught a glimpse of something—something moving just beyond the reach of the firelight. At first, it looked like a man, cloaked in darkness, but when Elias approached, it dissolved into the air like smoke. Since then, the shadows had followed him, lurking at the edge of his vision.

The storm was alive.

A faint rustling sound broke through his thoughts, and Elias turned sharply. A figure moved in the shadows near a cluster of old, withered trees. For a moment, he thought it was one of the villagers, but something about the way the figure moved made his instincts scream danger. The figure was too tall, too fluid, as if it was not entirely human.

Elias stepped forward, one hand on his sword, the other reaching for the dagger at his belt. His heartbeat quickened, but his expression remained calm. He had seen too much in his life to be easily frightened.

The figure took another step toward him, and the wind picked up, swirling leaves and dust around them. Elias's grip tightened on his blade. The storm seemed to react to the figure's presence, growing stronger, angrier.

"What do you want?" Elias called out, his voice steady, though tension coiled in his chest.

The figure stopped, standing still at the edge of the shadows. Then, in a voice barely above a whisper, it spoke. "*You cannot stop it. The storm will take everything.*"

Elias's blood ran cold. He had heard those words before—back in the ruined castle, whispered by the shadows that haunted his steps.

Before he could respond, the figure vanished, dissolving into the wind like mist. The storm roared to life behind him, dark clouds rolling in with terrifying speed. Thunder cracked overhead, and the village plunged into darkness.

# THE STORM OF SHADOWS

Elias stood alone at the edge of the storm; the weight of the prophecy heavy on his shoulders. He did not know who or what the figure was, but he did know one thing:

The *Storm of Shadows* had come for him.

And he was ready to face it.

# Chapter 2

The storm enveloped the village within minutes, swallowing the streets in an impenetrable blanket of darkness. Lightning cracked across the sky, casting fleeting shadows that danced along the walls of crumbling homes. The few villagers who had dared to stay outside scrambled for shelter, but Elias stood still, his eyes scanning the horizon.

Something was out there.

His grip tightened on his sword as he moved toward the heart of the village, his senses on high alert. The whispers returned, weaving through the wind, calling his name in a thousand voices that were neither near nor far.

"*Elias... Elias...*"

He shook his head, trying to dispel the eerie voices. He had to keep his mind clear. There was no time for fear, no time to dwell on the unknown. But the storm seemed alive with an intelligence, a malevolence that chilled him to the core. He could feel it watching, waiting.

As Elias approached the village square, a dim light flickered from within a rundown tavern. The sign above the door swung wildly in the wind, its worn lettering barely legible: *The Silver Mare*. The door creaked on its hinges, slamming open and shut in the gale, but a warm glow seeped out from inside.

With one last glance at the storm, Elias ducked into the tavern.

The moment he entered, the wind's howling became a dull roar, muffled by the thick wooden walls. Inside, the air was thick with the smell of burning wood and the sour stench of old ale. A few patrons

# THE STORM OF SHADOWS

huddled around a small fire in the hearth, their faces gaunt and lined with fear. They barely glanced up as Elias entered.

In the far corner, an old woman sat alone at a table, her hunched figure draped in tattered robes. Her eyes were milky white, clouded by age or blindness, but there was something unnerving about the way they seemed to follow him as he crossed the room. The whispers grew louder as he approached her, the wind outside rattling the windows as if trying to break in.

Elias hesitated. There was something about the old woman that did not belong here. She looked like a relic from a forgotten age, out of place among the trembling villagers. Her bony fingers clutched a wooden staff, and her lips moved as though she were whispering to herself, though no sound escaped them.

"You've come far," she said, her voice raspy and brittle, as if each word took immense effort.

Elias froze. The woman had not looked at him when she spoke, and yet there was no one else she could have been addressing.

"I've come because I have no choice," Elias replied, his voice low. He took a seat across from her, never letting his guard drop. "You know what's happening, don't you?"

The old woman's head tilted slightly, as if she were listening to something only, she could hear. Her lips curled into a knowing smile. "The storm... it calls for you. It has been waiting a long time."

Elias leaned forward, his eyes narrowing. "Why? What is it? Who controls it?"

The woman's eyes, though clouded, seemed to pierce through him. She did not answer immediately, instead raising a trembling hand to point at the window. "The storm is not just weather, boy. It is an ancient force, older than you or I. It is drawn to power... to blood."

Elias felt a chill creep up his spine. "What do you mean by blood?"

"The storm is alive because something within it gives it life. A shadow that once ruled this land, long before men built their cities. The storm is its herald, and it will not stop until it consumes everything."

He stared at her, trying to make sense of her words. "How do you know this?"

The old woman let out a harsh, dry laugh. "I have seen it before. When I was young, the storm came for my village too. It left nothing behind but ash and bones. I survived because I fled, but no one escapes the storm forever."

Her words hung in the air like a death sentence. Elias clenched his fists, frustration building inside him. He was no stranger to danger, but this was different—this was a force beyond anything he had faced before.

"There has to be a way to stop it," he said, his voice hardening with determination.

The woman's smile faded, replaced by a look of pity. "You cannot stop it. But you... you might survive it, if you are smart."

Elias shook his head. "I am not interested in survival. I want to know how to end this."

The old woman sighed, her frail body seeming to sink into her chair. "The storm follows the will of its master, and its master is bound to the *Shadowstone*. If you wish to end the storm, you must destroy the stone... or the one who wields it."

Elias frowned. "The Shadowstone?"

She nodded. "An ancient artifact, born of dark magic. It controls the shadows within the storm, binds them to the will of its owner. But beware, for the one who holds the stone is no mere man."

Elias felt the weight of her words, the enormity of the task before him. He had come seeking answers, and now he had them—though they were far more dangerous than he had imagined.

"Where do I find this stone?" he asked.

# THE STORM OF SHADOWS

The old woman leaned in, her voice barely above a whisper. "It lies in the heart of the storm, guarded by creatures that do not know death. You will need more than just your sword if you hope to face them."

As the wind howled outside, Elias knew that his journey was only just beginning. The storm was far more than a natural disaster—it was the work of something ancient, something evil. And now, it had set its sights on him.

The old woman's final words echoed in his mind as he rose from the table.

"Beware the shadows, Elias. They hunger for your soul."

With that, Elias stepped back into the storm, knowing that his fate was now tied to the darkness that hunted him.

# Chapter 3

The storm's fury raged as Elias stepped back into the wind-swept streets, the old woman's warning echoing in his mind. The whispers in the storm seemed to grow louder now, as if they were aware of his intentions—aware that he had learned of the *Shadowstone*. His cloak billowed around him, and his boots sank into the muddy earth as he pressed forward, determined to find his next move.

But the village was no longer the quiet, fearful place it had been moments ago. The storm was twisting it, reshaping the world around him. Shadows crawled across the cobblestones, taking on forms that slithered and darted through the wind. Elias caught fleeting glimpses of dark figures at the edges of his vision—figures that moved unnaturally fast, too silent for human feet.

The whispers called to him again, louder now. They swirled with the storm, blending with the howl of the wind. His name echoed through the dark, but now it was accompanied by something else: a pull, a magnetic force that seemed to tug at his very soul, urging him deeper into the storm's heart.

Elias took a deep breath and continued. If the *Shadowstone* was truly the key to stopping the storm, then he had no choice but to find it. But the old woman's words haunted him: *The one who holds the stone is no mere man.* He would need help—someone who knew how to fight the darkness that now surrounded him.

His instincts told him to head east, toward the wildlands where the storm seemed strongest. There, he hoped to find someone who could help him. Someone who understood the dark magic that fueled the storm.

# THE STORM OF SHADOWS

As Elias made his way through the village, the storm continued to worsen. Lightning flashed overhead, casting brief, blinding light over the desolate landscape. The shadows in the corners of his vision grew more pronounced, more aggressive. He could feel them watching him, waiting for the right moment to strike.

Then, as if on cue, the first attack came.

A figure lunged out of the shadows, moving faster than humanly possible. Its body was cloaked in darkness, its eyes glowing a sickly yellow. It had no face—just a smooth, black void where its features should have been. With a snarl, it slashed at Elias with claws made of pure shadow.

Elias barely had time to react. His sword came up just in time to parry the blow, sparks flying as steel met darkness. The creature recoiled, hissing as it circled him, its movements fluid and unnatural. More figures emerged from the shadows, surrounding him.

They were everywhere.

Elias gritted his teeth. He could not fight them all—not in this storm. The wind whipped around him, carrying the creatures' whispers on the air. They taunted him, hissed his name in mocking tones.

But Elias had faced worse odds before.

With a roar, he charged forward, slashing through the closest shadow with a powerful swing of his sword. The blade passed through the creature, and for a moment, it seemed to dissolve, but the shadows around it reformed instantly. He cursed under his breath. These creatures were not bound by the rules of the physical world.

Another shadow lunged, and Elias twisted, avoiding its attack. His dagger flew from his belt, embedding itself in the creature's chest. The impact knocked it back, but the darkness swirled around the blade, swallowing it whole.

The shadows were relentless.

Elias knew he could not keep this up forever. He needed an exit—some way to escape the horde of creatures that was growing larger by the second. His eyes scanned the village, searching for a path through the storm.

Then he saw it.

A figure stood at the far end of the street, cloaked in the storm's darkness. It was not one of the shadow creatures—this figure was taller, more human in its movements, though the storm seemed to part around it as if it were a part of the storm itself. In its hand, the figure held a staff that crackled with energy, glowing faintly against the backdrop of swirling chaos.

Without hesitation, Elias fought his way toward the figure. The shadows swarmed around him, clawing and slashing, but he pushed through, his sword flashing in the darkness. With each step, the storm seemed to grow angrier, as though it sensed he was getting closer to something—or someone—important.

Finally, he reached the figure.

Up close, Elias could see that it was a woman. Her face was hidden beneath a dark hood, but her eyes glowed with the same eerie light as the shadows. She did not move as he approached, simply watching him with an intensity that made his skin crawl.

"Who are you?" Elias demanded, his sword at the ready. "Why are you here?"

The woman's lips curled into a faint smile. "You are brave, to come this far into the storm. Few have made it as far as you."

Elias narrowed his eyes. "You didn't answer my question."

The woman's smile faded, and her gaze darkened. "I am Liora, and I have been tracking this storm for as long as I can remember. It calls to those who are bound to it. Those like you."

Elias blinked, caught off guard. "What do you mean, 'bound to it'?"

She stepped closer, her voice lowering to a near-whisper. "The storm is not just a force of nature. It is drawn to certain people—people with a connection to the *Shadowstone* and the magic it holds. You may not remember, but you have been bound to this storm long before you started chasing it."

Elias frowned. The idea made no sense, yet the more she spoke, the more a nagging feeling stirred within him—memories he could not quite place, shadows in his own mind that he had long ignored. "What are you talking about?"

Liora's gaze softened. "You have been touched by the same magic that fuels this storm. That is why it hunts you. That is why the shadows speak to you. They want to claim you... just like they claimed the others."

The storm raged around them, but for a moment, it seemed to quiet as Elias processed her words. He had always sensed something different about himself, something that set him apart from others. But this... this was far more than he had ever imagined.

"Then help me stop it," Elias said, his voice filled with grim determination. "If I am bound to it, I will use that connection to end this. I need to find the *Shadowstone*."

Liora studied him for a long moment before nodding. "Very well. But know this—once you enter the heart of the storm, there is no turning back. The shadows will not let you go a second time."

Elias met her gaze, his jaw set. "I don't intend to turn back."

With that, the two of them stepped into the swirling darkness, heading deeper into the storm's deadly embrace.

# Chapter 4

The storm closed in around Elias and Liora as they ventured deeper into its core. The wind, now a constant roar, seemed to move with purpose, directing them toward an unknown destination. The shadows, once chaotic and scattered, had become more organized, flowing like a living entity just beyond their reach. It felt as if the storm was watching, waiting for the right moment to strike.

Liora walked in silence beside Elias, her staff glowing faintly in the dark, a beacon of light in the swirling tempest. Every now and then, her eyes darted to the side, tracking the movement of the shadows with a calm focus that Elias envied. She seemed to know exactly where they were going, her steps never faltering despite the chaos around them.

"What's waiting for us?" Elias asked after a long silence, his voice barely audible over the howling wind.

Liora did not turn to him, her eyes fixed ahead. "The heart of the storm," she said. "The place where the *Shadowstone* lies. It is not a place for the living, Elias. The shadows there are stronger, more dangerous. If we are not careful, we will not leave."

Elias nodded, his grip tightening on the hilt of his sword. He had expected as much. There was no easy path in this journey, but he had come too far to turn back now. The storm had already taken too much from him—his peace, his purpose, and nearly his sanity. He would not let it win.

They walked for what felt like hours, though time had lost meaning in the storm. The village was long behind them, swallowed by the tempest, and now they were in an endless expanse of darkness. There were no landmarks, no roads—only the swirling shadows and the

# THE STORM OF SHADOWS

relentless wind. Every step felt heavier, as if the storm itself was pushing back against them.

Elias glanced at Liora. "How do you know the way?"

Liora's expression remained unreadable as she answered. "The storm calls to me, just as it does to you. I have followed its whispers for years, but it always kept me at arm's length. Now, with you here, the path is clearer."

He frowned. "What do you mean 'with me here'? You said the storm was drawn to me. Why?"

Liora hesitated, her gaze flickering for just a moment. "You are more connected to the *Shadowstone* than you realize, Elias. The magic that binds the storm to this world is ancient, and it seeks out those who have a part to play in its fate. Whether you were chosen for this or stumbled upon it does not matter now. The storm knows you. It has been waiting for you."

Elias clenched his jaw, the weight of her words sinking in. He had always felt the pull of something dark, something beyond his understanding, but he had never questioned it—never dug deeper. Now, it seemed, there was no avoiding it. He had been bound to this storm long before he knew it existed.

Suddenly, the wind died down, and the storm around them shifted. The howling ceased, replaced by an eerie silence that was more unsettling than the noise. Elias stopped, his eyes narrowing as he scanned the area. The shadows were no longer moving—they were still, like predators waiting to pounce.

Liora stopped beside him, her staff glowing brighter. "We're close," she whispered, her voice tense. "Be ready."

The ground beneath them trembled, and the air grew thick with an oppressive energy. Elias could feel it—the pull of the *Shadowstone*, drawing him closer with every step. His heartbeat quickened, but he forced himself to remain calm. He could not afford to lose focus now.

They walked into a clearing, where the storm's swirling mass seemed to part, revealing the heart of the darkness. In the center of the clearing stood an ancient stone monolith, black as night, pulsating with a deep, malevolent energy. Surrounding it were the shadow creatures, dozens of them, their glowing eyes fixed on the intruders.

The *Shadowstone*.

Elias felt its power immediately. It was not just magic—it was something older, something primal. The stone hummed with dark energy; its surface etched with runes that glowed faintly in the storm's light. The shadows that surrounded it were like an army, guardians of the stone, waiting for the order to attack.

Liora stepped forward, her staff raised. "This is it," she said, her voice steady despite the overwhelming darkness. "Once the stone is destroyed, the storm will lose its power. But the shadows will not let us get close."

Elias nodded, his sword already in his hand. "Then we fight."

The moment the words left his mouth, the shadows lunged.

The first creature came at him fast, its claws aimed for his throat. Elias parried the attack, his blade slicing through the creature's form. It dissolved into smoke, but more followed, swarming him from all sides. The shadows were relentless, their movements faster, more aggressive than before.

Elias fought with everything he had, his sword a blur of motion as he cut down one creature after another. But for every shadow he destroyed, two more seemed to take its place. The creatures were unending, a manifestation of the storm's wrath.

Liora stood beside him, her staff crackling with energy as she sent blasts of light into the horde. Each pulse of magic sent shadows scattering, but they regrouped quickly, reforming and attacking with renewed fury. Sweat dripped down Elias's face as he fought, his muscles burning with exhaustion.

# THE STORM OF SHADOWS

"This isn't working," Elias shouted over the din of battle. "We're being overwhelmed!"

Liora's eyes narrowed as she unleashed another blast of energy. "We need to get to the stone. It is the only way."

Elias knew she was right. Fighting the shadows would only delay the inevitable. The source of the storm's power was the *Shadowstone*, and until it was destroyed, the storm would continue to rage.

With a roar, Elias charged toward the monolith, cutting through the shadows that blocked his path. His blade moved with precision, slicing through the darkness as he fought his way closer. Liora followed, her staff glowing brighter with each step.

As they neared the stone, the air grew colder, and the ground trembled beneath their feet. The shadows seemed to sense their intent, swarming around the stone in a desperate attempt to protect it.

Elias reached the base of the *Shadowstone* and raised his sword, ready to strike. But before he could bring the blade down, a figure materialized in front of him—a tall, imposing figure cloaked in shadows, its face obscured by darkness.

The master of the storm.

The figure raised a hand, and the shadows around it surged forward, knocking Elias back with a force that sent him crashing to the ground. Pain shot through his body as he struggled to stand, but the figure was already moving, its hand reaching for the *Shadowstone*.

Liora unleashed a blast of magic, but the figure deflected it with a wave of its hand, the energy dissipating into the storm. The figure turned toward Elias, its eyes glowing with an unnatural light.

"You are too late," the figure said, its voice echoing with the sound of the storm. "The stone's power is eternal. You cannot stop it."

Elias gritted his teeth, his hand tightening around the hilt of his sword. He was not going to let the storm win—not now, not ever.

With a final surge of strength, Elias lunged at the figure, his sword aimed at the *Shadowstone*. The figure moved to block him, but Elias was faster, his blade striking the stone with all his might.

The moment his sword made lo contact; the stone shattered.

A deafening roar filled the air as the storm erupted in fury, the shadows around them dissolving into nothingness. The figure let out a scream of rage as it too began to fade, its form unraveling in the wake of the stone's destruction. The storm was breaking.

Elias fell to his knees, gasping for breath as the wind died down and the darkness began to lift. Liora stood beside him, her eyes wide with disbelief.

"It's over," she whispered.

But as the last remnants of the storm faded, Elias knew that their journey was far from finished. The storm may have been defeated, but the darkness behind it was still out there, waiting.

And it would return.

# Chapter 5

The storm had broken, but the world around Elias and Liora still felt unnaturally quiet. The air was thick with the residue of dark magic, a reminder that the battle was far from over. As the last remnants of the storm faded into the horizon, Elias remained kneeling on the cold ground, staring at the shattered fragments of the *Shadowstone*. His body ached from the effort, and his mind was still reeling from the encounter with the shadowed figure.

Liora stood beside him, her staff still glowing faintly. She scanned the clearing, her expression tense. "It's gone... but something isn't right," she murmured. "This was too easy."

Elias gritted his teeth. "Easy?" he said, standing slowly. "I almost got killed back there, and you call that easy?"

Liora turned to him, her eyes serious. "The *Shadowstone* was powerful, yes. But this storm was not natural. It was controlled—created by something far more dangerous than we have seen."

Her words hung in the air, and Elias felt a chill crawl up his spine. He had sensed it too—the feeling that they were being manipulated, drawn into a fight that was not truly over. The shadowed figure, the one who had defended the stone, was not just a guardian. It was a part of something larger.

"We need answers," Elias said, brushing the dirt from his cloak. "If the storm was just a part of something bigger, then what are we dealing with?"

Liora hesitated, her gaze flickering toward the distance. "I do not know yet. But I do know someone who might."

Elias raised an eyebrow. "Who?"

Without answering, Liora turned and began walking toward the edge of the clearing, her pace quick and purposeful. "We need to find someone who can speak to the shadows," she called over her shoulder. "Someone who knows their language."

Elias followed, confused and weary. "I thought we just destroyed the source of the shadows."

Liora shook her head. "No. The *Shadowstone* was only a fragment of the power behind the storm. The real threat lies in the magic that created it. And that magic is old—older than anything you have ever known."

They traveled through the night, leaving the shattered remains of the stone behind. The path was difficult, but Elias kept his eyes on Liora as she led the way. She moved with a silent determination, and though she did not say much, her mind was clearly racing with thoughts Elias could not begin to guess.

As they neared the outskirts of the wildlands, a dense fog began to roll in, obscuring their surroundings. The trees were gnarled and twisted, their branches like skeletal fingers reaching for the sky. The ground was soft beneath their feet, and the air grew colder with every step.

"Where are we going?" Elias asked, breaking the silence.

Liora paused, turning to face him. "There is an old temple hidden deep within the wildlands. It is a place where dark magic was once practiced, long before the kingdoms rose. If we are lucky, we will find a man there who can help us."

Elias frowned. "And who exactly is this man?"

"He's a scholar," Liora explained. "Someone who spent years studying the ancient languages of shadow magic. If anyone knows what is behind this storm, it is him."

Elias was not convinced. "A scholar? Are we really trusting some old man who has been hiding in a temple for gods know how long?"

# THE STORM OF SHADOWS

Liora smiled faintly. "You will see. He is more than just a scholar."

After hours of trekking through the fog-covered forest, they finally reached the temple. It was a crumbling ruin, its once-grand stone pillars now covered in moss and vines. The entrance was partially collapsed, but a faint glow emanated from within, casting an eerie light over the surrounding area.

Elias hesitated at the threshold. "This doesn't look welcoming."

Liora stepped forward without hesitation. "It's not meant to be."

They entered the temple, the air inside heavy with the scent of damp stone and ancient magic. The glow came from torches along the walls, flickering with an unnatural, bluish flame. The shadows here seemed to cling to the corners, watching, waiting.

At the far end of the temple, seated on a worn stone chair, was a figure cloaked in dark robes. His face was hidden in shadow, but the moment they approached, he lifted his head, revealing deep-set eyes that glimmered with knowledge—and something more unsettling.

"Liora," the man said in a low, rasping voice. "It's been a long time."

Liora inclined her head. "Too long, Zorin."

Zorin stood slowly; his movements deliberate. He was tall, his presence commanding despite his thin, almost fragile appearance. His hands, thin and bony, rested on a staff that seemed to pulse with the same unnatural energy as the torches.

Elias felt the hairs on the back of his neck stand on end.

"You've come for answers," Zorin said, his eyes shifting to Elias. "I can see the questions in your mind. The storm... the shadows... they all lead back to something far older than you could ever imagine."

Elias stepped forward, his expression hard. "What do you know about the storm?"

Zorin smiled faintly, though there was no warmth in it. "The storm was merely a herald. A warning of what is to come. The *Shadowstone* was but a tool, a relic of an ancient war. But the true power behind the storm... that is something far worse."

Liora's eyes narrowed. "What are we dealing with, Zorin?"

Zorin's gaze darkened, and the torches seemed to flicker in response. "The storm was conjured by an entity known as *The Harbinger*. A creature born of the darkest magic, once imprisoned long ago. But now, the seals that held it are weakening."

Elias felt a cold knot form in his stomach. "How do we stop it?"

Zorin's eyes gleamed with a dangerous light. "Stop it? You do not stop something like *The Harbinger*. You can only delay it. But to do that, you must first understand its origins. You must go where the darkness began."

Elias's mind raced. "And where is that?"

Zorin leaned forward, his voice barely a whisper. "The Forgotten City—buried beneath the sands of time. That is where the darkness first took root, and where you will find what you seek."

Liora's expression remained calm, but Elias could see the concern in her eyes.

"Are you ready for this, Elias?" she asked quietly.

Elias glanced at her, then back at Zorin. His thoughts were a whirl of doubt, fear, and determination. But he knew there was no turning back now.

"I have no choice," he said.

Zorin smiled again, this time with genuine amusement. "Then may the shadows guide your path."

# Chapter 6

The temple's eerie glow faded behind them as Elias and Liora made their way deeper into the wildlands. The shadows of the ancient forest pressed in around them, twisting trees and vines like the arms of forgotten gods. Every step felt heavier, as though the air itself was thick with the weight of untold history. Zorin's words echoed in Elias's mind—*The Forgotten City*, buried beneath sands and time, hiding the truth of the storm and the ancient creature known as *The Harbinger*.

Elias could not shake the feeling of dread that had settled over him since leaving the temple. They were no longer fighting just shadows; they were facing something far more sinister—something that had been waiting in the darkness for centuries.

"How far is the Forgotten City?" Elias asked, breaking the silence that had stretched between them.

Liora did not look back as she answered. "Days, if we are lucky. Weeks, if we are not."

Elias frowned. "And if we're not lucky?"

Liora's voice was calm, but there was an edge to it. "Then the wildlands will swallow us whole before we ever get there."

Elias glanced around, feeling the oppressive nature of the wildlands closing in. He had heard stories of this place—a land forgotten by time, where the rules of the natural world no longer applied. Creatures lurked in the shadows, and ancient magic still flowed beneath the ground like rivers of darkness.

As if sensing his thoughts, Liora spoke again. "The wildlands are dangerous, but they are also alive. They remember. If we can navigate through them, we might find more than just the Forgotten City. We could uncover the history that has been lost to the world."

Elias walked in silence for a moment, contemplating her words. "What exactly are we looking for in this city? Zorin did not give us much."

Liora's eyes narrowed slightly. "We are not just looking for the city, Elias. We are looking for the origins of the storm, of *The Harbinger*. Zorin mentioned that the darkness took root there, which means there is something in that city that started all of this—something that can help us understand how to stop it."

Elias exhaled, the weight of their quest settling heavily on his shoulders. "And if we don't find it?"

Liora did not answer, but the silence that followed spoke volumes. They both knew that failure was not an option. The storm's destruction had been a temporary victory, but if *The Harbinger* was truly free, the real battle had yet to begin.

**Nightfall**

As the sun dipped below the horizon, the wildlands grew darker and more foreboding. The temperature dropped, and the wind howled through the trees, carrying with it strange sounds—whispers, like distant voices carried on the wind.

"We need to stop for the night," Liora said, her voice steady despite the growing tension. "The wildlands become even more dangerous after dark."

Elias nodded, though the idea of stopping did not sit well with him. Something about this place made his skin crawl, as though they were being watched from the shadows.

They found a small clearing, and Liora quickly set up wards with her staff, creating a protective circle of light around them. The pale glow pushed back the darkness, but Elias could still feel the weight of the forest pressing in from beyond the circle's edge.

# THE STORM OF SHADOWS

As they sat beside a small fire, Liora pulled out a map—ancient and worn, the edges frayed with time. She spread it across the ground, her eyes scanning the faded markings.

"This is where we are," she said, pointing to a small mark near the edge of the map. "The Forgotten City lies to the southeast, but there are obstacles along the way—cursed ruins, corrupted forests, and worse."

Elias leaned over the map, tracing the path with his eyes. "We'll have to go through each of them, won't we?"

Liora nodded. "There is no other way. The city is buried deep within the heart of the wildlands, and the magic that protects it is older than the kingdoms themselves."

Elias sat back, rubbing his temples. "Great. So, we are walking into a death trap."

Liora smiled faintly. "It is not a trap if you know where the danger is. And I have navigated these wildlands before. With me, we have a chance."

Elias was not sure whether to feel reassured or more concerned. Liora was confident, but even she could not control what awaited them in the depths of the wildlands. As they prepared to rest, he could not shake the feeling that something was watching them, just beyond the light.

**Dreams of the Past**

That night, Elias dreamed.

He stood in the center of an ancient city, its buildings towering over him like monoliths. The streets were empty, the air thick with the scent of decay and forgotten time. Shadows moved through the alleyways, but they were different from the ones he had fought—these were older, more primal.

In the distance, he could hear the soft hum of the *Shadowstone*, but it was faint, as though it was calling from the depths of the earth. The city itself seemed alive, pulsing with a dark energy that made his skin tingle.

Suddenly, a figure appeared before him—a tall, cloaked man with eyes like burning coals. The man's presence was suffocating, his aura dripping with power and malice.

"You think you can stop it?" the figure whispered, his voice echoing through the empty streets. "The storm was just the beginning. The darkness behind it will consume everything."

Elias tried to speak, but his voice caught in his throat. He felt a pull toward the figure, as though some unseen force was drawing him closer.

The figure smiled, a cold, cruel grin. "The Harbinger is awake. And it remembers you."

With that, the dream shattered, and Elias woke with a gasp, his heart pounding in his chest. The fire had died down, and the forest was eerily silent. Liora sat nearby, her eyes closed in meditation, but she must have sensed his distress, because she opened them and looked at him.

"Another dream?" she asked softly.

Elias nodded, wiping the sweat from his brow. "It was... different this time. I saw a city, and a figure—someone powerful. He said The Harbinger remembers me."

Liora's expression darkened. "It is already reaching out to you. The closer we get to the Forgotten City, the stronger its influence will become."

Elias swallowed hard; the weight of his dream still heavy in his mind. "What do we do?"

Liora stood, her staff glowing faintly. "We keep moving. The longer we stay here, the more vulnerable we are. The wildlands feed on fear and hesitation."

Elias stood as well, gripping his sword tightly. As they packed up camp and prepared to continue their journey, the weight of the coming darkness pressed down on him.

Whatever awaited them in the Forgotten City, Elias knew it was something far worse than he had ever imagined.

## THE STORM OF SHADOWS

And it was waiting for him.

# Chapter 7

The following days were a blur of movement as Elias and Liora pushed deeper into the wildlands. The air grew colder, and the trees loomed larger, casting long, dark shadows over their path. Even the ground felt different, softer, and spongier, as though it were absorbing the life around it. Every step seemed heavier than the last, the weight of the land itself growing oppressive.

The silence in the wildlands was unnatural. There were no sounds of wildlife, no rustling leaves, no distant howls—just the eerie, constant hush that surrounded them. And yet, Elias could not shake the feeling that something was watching them from the shadows, waiting for the right moment to strike.

"How much farther?" Elias asked, breaking the silence.

Liora did not slow her pace, but her voice was steady when she replied, "We are close. Maybe another day, if we are not delayed."

Elias looked ahead at the seemingly endless expanse of trees and fog. "Delayed by what?"

Before Liora could answer, the ground beneath their feet shifted, and a low rumble echoed through the forest. The air suddenly grew colder, and Elias felt the unmistakable sensation of magic swirling around them. The shadows that clung to the trees seemed to shift and pulse with life.

Liora raised her staff, the soft glow of its light intensifying. "Something's coming."

The rumble grew louder, and from the fog ahead, dark shapes began to emerge. At first, they were formless—black masses of shadow that slithered along the ground. But as they drew closer, they took on more distinct forms: humanoid figures with hollow eyes and twisted, gaunt bodies, their features barely discernible beneath the writhing shadows that cloaked them.

"The Wraiths," Liora muttered. "They're drawn to the magic in this place."

Elias gripped his sword tightly, his heart pounding. He had fought creatures of shadow before, but these were different. There was something deeply unsettling about the Wraiths—something that made his blood run cold.

"How do we fight them?" he asked, glancing at Liora.

"They can't be killed," she said, her eyes fixed on the approaching figures. "Not in the traditional sense. We must drive them back with light. Stay close to me."

Elias nodded, his grip tightening on his sword. He could feel the darkness pressing in around them, the Wraiths advancing slowly but steadily, their hollow eyes fixed on him.

Liora raised her staff, and with a flick of her wrist, a blinding light erupted from its tip, cutting through the fog, and illuminating the forest. The Wraiths recoiled, their bodies writhing and hissing as they were forced back by the light. But even as they retreated, more appeared from the shadows, undeterred by the magic.

"We can't stay here," Liora said, her voice strained. "The light will only hold them off for so long."

Elias did not need any more encouragement. "Let's move!"

They ran through the forest, the ground shifting and trembling beneath their feet as the Wraiths closed in from all sides. Liora kept her staff raised, casting light in every direction, but the creatures were relentless, their forms slithering through the darkness like smoke.

Elias could hear their whispers now—soft, chilling voices that echoed in his mind, filling his thoughts with doubt and fear.

*"You cannot escape... You will join us... You belong to the shadows..."*

He gritted his teeth, shaking off the voices as best he could. But they grew louder, more insistent, filling his mind with images of darkness and death.

"Liora!" he called, his voice tinged with panic. "They're getting inside my head!"

Liora did not turn, but her voice was urgent. "Focus, Elias! Do not let them in! The shadows feed on fear—do not give them anything to hold on to!"

Elias nodded, trying to push the whispers from his mind, but it was difficult. The Wraiths were closing in, their forms twisting and shifting as they moved through the fog, their hollow eyes fixed on him. He could feel their presence in his mind, tugging at his thoughts, filling him with dread.

Suddenly, the ground beneath them gave way, and they were plunged into darkness.

**The Chasm**

Elias hit the ground hard, the air knocked from his lungs as he tumbled down a steep slope. The world spun around him, and for a moment, he lost all sense of direction. His sword clattered away into the darkness, and he reached out desperately, trying to find something to grab onto.

Finally, he came to a stop, his body aching from the fall. He groaned, rolling onto his back and staring up at the dark sky above. The fog swirled overhead, and the faint glow of Liora's staff was the only light in the darkness.

"Elias!" Liora's voice echoed from above. "Are you all right?"

Elias coughed, sitting up slowly. "I am alive. Barely."

He glanced around, his eyes adjusting to the darkness. They had fallen into a deep chasm, the walls towering above them like jagged cliffs. The Wraiths were nowhere to be seen, but he could still feel their presence lurking in the shadows.

# THE STORM OF SHADOWS

Liora carefully made her way down the slope, her staff illuminating the path. When she reached him, she offered a hand to help him to his feet.

"We have to keep moving," she said, her voice calm but urgent. "The Wraiths won't give up so easily."

Elias nodded, still shaken from the fall. "Where are we?"

Liora glanced around, her eyes scanning the walls of the chasm. "This is part of the old forest—there are caverns beneath the wildlands. We might be able to find a way through them."

Elias retrieved his sword, gripping it tightly as they started walking deeper into the chasm. The air was thick with moisture, and the walls of the cavern were slick with moss and water. The light from Liora's staff cast long shadows that danced across the stone, creating an eerie atmosphere.

As they moved deeper, the whispers returned, faint but persistent, echoing off the walls of the cavern.

*"You cannot escape... You will fall into darkness..."*

Elias clenched his jaw, trying to focus on the path ahead. But the whispers grew louder with every step, filling the cavern with their eerie, disembodied voices. He could feel the weight of the darkness pressing down on him, suffocating, as though the shadows were alive and reaching for him.

"We're close," Liora said suddenly, her voice cutting through the whispers.

Elias looked up, frowning. "Close to what?"

Liora stopped, turning to face him. Her eyes were intense, her expression grim. "The entrance to the Forgotten City."

Elias's heart skipped a beat. "Already?"

Liora nodded, her gaze shifting to a large, stone archway carved into the side of the cavern. It was ancient, covered in moss and cracked with age, but there was no mistaking its purpose.

"This is where the darkness began," Liora said quietly. "And where we'll find the answers, we seek."

Elias stared at the archway, his mind racing. The Forgotten City lay just beyond it, hidden beneath the wildlands for centuries. But now that they had found it, he could not shake the feeling that they were walking into something far worse than they had ever imagined.

The shadows seemed to thicken around the archway, as though they were guarding it, waiting for someone to step through and awaken whatever lay inside.

Liora took a deep breath, her hand tightening on her staff. "Are you ready?"

Elias hesitated for a moment, the weight of everything they had faced—and everything still to come—pressing down on him. But there was no turning back now. Whatever lay in the Forgotten City, they had to face it.

He nodded, gripping his sword tightly. "Let's go."

Together, they stepped through the archway and into the heart of the darkness.

# Chapter 8

The moment Elias and Liora stepped through the archway, the air grew thick, charged with a powerful magic that pulsed through the stone walls. It was as if the city itself was alive, breathing in the dark energy that had lain dormant for centuries. The whispers faded, replaced by an unsettling silence that only deepened the tension.

Elias gazed around in awe. The Forgotten City sprawled before them, ancient and decayed, its towering structures looming like shadows in the dim light of Liora's staff. Massive stone buildings, cracked and overgrown with vines, lined the narrow streets. The architecture was unlike anything Elias had ever seen—sharp angles, intricate carvings, and statues that seemed to watch them with hollow eyes. Even in ruin, the city was awe-inspiring.

But something was wrong. The air was too still, too quiet, as if the city had been waiting for them.

"We're here," Liora whispered, her voice almost drowned by the heavy silence. She seemed lost in thought, her eyes scanning the darkened streets. "This place... it's been untouched for centuries."

Elias nodded, gripping his sword tighter. "Where do we start?"

Liora pointed toward the heart of the city, where a massive tower rose above the rest of the buildings. It was cracked and weathered, but it still stood tall, defying time and decay.

"The central tower," she said. "That is where we will find what we are looking for. If there is any clue about how to stop The Harbinger, it will be there."

Elias glanced at the tower, feeling a chill run down his spine. "And what if The Harbinger is waiting for us inside?"

Liora met his gaze, her expression grim. "Then we'll face it together."

They began making their way through the abandoned streets, their footsteps echoing eerily in the silence. As they moved deeper into the city, Elias could not shake the feeling that they were being watched. The statues that lined the streets seemed to follow their every move, their empty eyes tracking them as they passed. Shadows shifted unnaturally, clinging to the walls and ground like living things.

"Liora," Elias said, his voice hushed. "What exactly happened here? Why was this city abandoned?"

Liora's expression darkened. "The Forgotten City was once a thriving center of knowledge and magic. The people here were some of the most powerful sorcerers in the world. But something went wrong. Legends say they tampered with dark magic—something ancient, something that was never meant to be touched. And when they unleashed it, the city fell into ruin. The storm began here."

Elias shivered. "And now we're walking into the heart of it."

Liora nodded. "We need to know what they found. It is the only way to understand The Harbinger's power."

**The Tower**

As they reached the base of the towering structure, a wave of unease washed over Elias. The door to the tower was cracked open, a faint light spilling out from within, casting long shadows across the ground. The stone steps leading up to the entrance were worn and weathered, but they showed signs of recent use—scuff marks and footprints in the dust.

"Someone's been here," Elias said, his voice low.

Liora's eyes narrowed. "Or something."

They exchanged a glance, and without another word, they climbed the steps. The door creaked as they pushed it open, revealing a vast, circular chamber beyond. The room was lit by a strange, ethereal glow that seemed to emanate from the walls themselves. Shelves lined with

## THE STORM OF SHADOWS

ancient tomes and scrolls stretched up toward the ceiling, and in the center of the room stood a massive stone pedestal, upon which rested a glowing crystal—pulsing faintly with dark energy.

Elias felt his breath catch in his throat. "What is that?"

Liora's eyes were wide with a mixture of awe and fear. "The Shadowstone."

Elias took a cautious step closer, the pull of the stone's dark energy almost irresistible. The whispers that had followed them through the wildlands began to return, faint at first, but growing louder the closer he got to the stone.

Liora stepped forward, her hand outstretched toward the stone. "This is it, Elias. This is the source of The Harbinger's power."

Elias frowned. "What do you mean? This stone... it is what created the storm?"

Liora nodded. "The sorcerers of the Forgotten City found this stone deep beneath the earth. They did not understand its power, but they tried to harness it. The storm was a byproduct of their failure, but the real danger is the stone itself. It is connected to The Harbinger. It *is* The Harbinger."

Elias stepped back, his heart racing. "So, what do we do? Destroy it?"

Liora shook her head. "No. We cannot destroy it—not yet. If we do, we risk releasing The Harbinger in its full form. We need to find a way to contain it, to sever its connection to the darkness."

Before Elias could respond, the room suddenly trembled, and a low growl echoed from the shadows. The temperature plummeted, and the air grew thick with an unnatural cold.

"We're not alone," Elias said, his voice tense.

From the shadows at the edge of the chamber, a figure emerged—tall, cloaked in darkness, with burning eyes that pierced through the gloom. It was the same figure Elias had seen in his dream, the one who had whispered of The Harbinger's awakening.

"You've come far, but you are too late," the figure said, its voice a cold, hollow rasp. "The Harbinger is already free."

Elias gripped his sword, his pulse quickening. "Who are you?"

The figure smiled, a cold, cruel grin. "I am the Keeper of Shadows. I serve The Harbinger. And soon, you will too."

Elias stepped forward; his sword raised. "We won't let that happen."

The Keeper of Shadows laughed, a sound that sent chills down Elias's spine. "You think you can stop it? You think you can stand against the darkness that consumes all?"

Liora's staff flared with light, cutting through the shadows. "We'll do whatever it takes."

The Keeper's eyes narrowed. "Then you will die here, like the sorcerers before you."

With a flick of his hand, the shadows in the room surged forward, swirling around Elias and Liora like a storm. Elias swung his sword, cutting through the darkness, but the shadows seemed endless, coiling around him, and pulling him down.

Liora stood her ground, her staff glowing brightly as she fought to push back the darkness. But the Keeper was powerful, and the shadows only grew stronger.

"We need to get to the stone!" Liora shouted, her voice strained. "It's the only way to stop him!"

Elias fought his way through the swirling darkness, his sword cutting through the tendrils of shadow that tried to drag him down. He reached the stone, his hand hovering over it.

"What do I do?" he called out to Liora.

"Touch it!" she cried. "You have to sever the connection!"

Without hesitation, Elias placed his hand on the stone. A surge of dark energy shot through him, and for a moment, he was overwhelmed by the power of the shadows—the whispers, the fear, the cold.

But then, something inside him pushed back, a light that had been buried deep within him since the storm had first begun. He focused on that light, channeling it through his hand and into the stone.

The room shook violently, and the shadows screamed, writhing in agony as the connection between the stone and The Harbinger was severed. The Keeper of Shadows let out a furious roar, his form disintegrating into smoke as the power that had sustained him was ripped away.

The stone shattered beneath Elias's hand, sending shards of dark energy spiraling into the air.

And then, there was silence.

**Aftermath**

Elias stumbled back, breathing heavily. The shadows had vanished, and the cold, oppressive air had lifted. The chamber was still, the only sound the crackling of the shattered stone at his feet.

Liora lowered her staff, her face pale but determined. "You did it."

Elias stared at the shards of the Shadowstone, his heart still racing. "But is it over?"

Liora shook her head. "No. The Harbinger is still out there, but its power has been weakened. We have bought ourselves time."

Elias exhaled slowly, the weight of their journey settling on his shoulders. "What now?"

Liora's eyes were filled with resolve. "Now, we prepare for the final battle."

As they left the chamber and made their way back through the city, Elias could not shake the feeling that this was only the beginning. The Harbinger had been weakened, but it was not defeated.

And soon, the storm of shadows would return.

As they made their way out of the tower, the oppressive weight of the shadows had lifted, but the silence of the Forgotten City still pressed down on them. Elias glanced over his shoulder, half-expecting the shadows to reappear, but the streets remained empty. The ancient buildings loomed like sentinels; their stone faces frozen in time.

Liora walked ahead, her staff still glowing faintly, though its light was no longer a beacon against the darkness. She moved with purpose, but Elias could see the weariness in her steps.

"We may have weakened the stone, but I can still feel the remnants of its power," Liora said, her voice soft but steady. "The city isn't as it once was, but it's not completely free from the influence of the shadows."

Elias frowned. "Do you think the Harbinger's forces will return?"

Liora paused, turning to face him. Her violet eyes, usually so calm, now reflected the weight of their journey. "The Harbinger is weakened, but not defeated. It will regroup, and when it does, the storm will rise again. We have bought ourselves time, but not much. We need to be ready."

Elias nodded, feeling the heaviness of that truth settle in his chest. "How do we prepare for something like that? The Harbinger... It is more than just a creature. It is like a force of nature, like a living storm."

Liora glanced back toward the shattered remains of the Shadowstone. "We do not have all the answers yet, but we do know that the Harbinger draws its power from fear and despair. The more chaos and destruction it creates, the stronger it becomes. If we can cut off its source of power, we stand a chance."

Elias thought about the devastation they had already witnessed—the lands ravaged by the storm; the people driven to madness by the whispers. "How do we stop that? How do we stop something that feeds on the very fear it creates?"

Liora looked away, her expression unreadable. "We need to find the origin of its power. The Shadowstone was only a fragment of a larger whole. Somewhere, deep in the wildlands or perhaps beyond, there is a source—the heart of the darkness itself. We must destroy it before the Harbinger can restore its full strength."

Elias's grip tightened on his sword. "And where do we even begin to look for something like that?"

Liora took a deep breath, her gaze distant. "The legends speak of an ancient temple, hidden far beneath the mountains to the north. It is said to be the birthplace of the first shadow, where the lines between this world and the other realms blur. If the Harbinger's heart is anywhere, it will be there."

Elias raised an eyebrow. "That sounds... ominous."

Liora offered a faint smile. "It is. But it is our only chance."

**The Weight of the Past**

As they began their journey out of the Forgotten City, Elias found himself lost in thought. The battles they had fought, the secrets they had uncovered, and the sacrifices they had made—it was all leading to this final confrontation. But despite the progress they had made, he could not shake the feeling that they were still walking into the unknown.

They had barely scratched the surface of the Harbinger's true power, and Elias wondered if they would be strong enough to face what lay ahead.

Liora's voice broke through his thoughts. "You've been quiet."

Elias shrugged, forcing a half-smile. "Just thinking about what is next. Every time we face one of these challenges, I wonder if we are getting closer to victory or just delaying the inevitable."

Liora slowed her pace, her eyes softening as she looked at him. "It is natural to have doubts. I feel them too. But you have proven time and again that you are stronger than you realize. You have faced the darkness head-on and survived. That is more than most can say."

Elias met her gaze, grateful for her words, but the weight of the responsibility still sat heavily on his shoulders. "But what if it is not enough? What if we fail?"

Liora stopped and placed a hand on his arm, her touch light but reassuring. "We will not fail, Elias. Not because we are invincible, but because we know what is at stake. We are fighting for more than just ourselves. We are fighting for the people who cannot fight, for those who are lost in the storm. That is what gives us strength."

Elias nodded, her words resonating with him. She was right—they could not afford to give in to despair. Not when so many lives depended on them. He took a deep breath, steeling himself for what was to come.

"We'll find the temple," he said, his voice firm. "And we'll end this."

Liora's eyes sparkled with determination. "Together."

## THE SHADOWS LINGER

As they reached the edge of the city, the sky above began to darken once more. The swirling clouds of the storm, though distant, still loomed on the horizon, a reminder of the danger that lingered just beyond their grasp.

Elias cast one last look at the Forgotten City, the ruins of a once-great civilization now lost to time and darkness. The Keeper of Shadows was gone, but the memory of his cold, burning eyes haunted Elias's mind.

He turned to Liora. "Do you think there is any hope for this place? For the people who once lived here?"

Liora's expression was somber. "The Forgotten City is a cautionary tale—a reminder of the dangers of unchecked power. The people here tried to control forces they did not understand, and they paid the price. But perhaps, one day, when the darkness is truly gone, this city can be reborn."

Elias nodded, though part of him doubted it would ever be the same. Some scars, especially those left by magic, never truly healed.

They continued walking, the shadows of the Forgotten City slowly fading behind them. Ahead, the path stretched toward the distant mountains, where the temple of shadows waited for them.

# THE STORM OF SHADOWS

## A Glimpse of the Future

As the day wore on, they found a small clearing to rest for the night. The storm remained on the horizon, distant but ever-present, its dark clouds swirling like a slow-moving tide.

Elias sat by the fire, staring into the flames. His mind drifted to thoughts of the future—the final battle, the looming confrontation with the Harbinger, and what might come after. He could not help but wonder if they would survive, if they would ever see the world at peace again.

Liora sat beside him, her eyes reflecting the flickering light of the fire. She spoke softly, almost as if reading his thoughts. "It's hard not to think about what comes next, isn't it?"

Elias nodded. "Yeah. I keep thinking about what will happen if we win. What will the world look like without the storm? Without the fear?"

Liora smiled, though there was a hint of sadness in her eyes. "A world without the storm... It is hard to imagine. But that is why we must keep fighting. Because that world is worth everything we have been through."

Elias leaned back, staring up at the stars that peeked through the clouds. "Do you think we will ever get there? To that world?"

Liora's gaze followed his. "I think... as long as we keep believing in it, there's always a chance."

For a moment, the weight of the journey ahead lifted, and they sat in silence, the fire crackling softly between them. The world they dreamed of—one without shadows, without the Harbinger's darkness—seemed distant but not impossible.

And as the fire burned low, Elias made a silent vow to see it through to the end, no matter the cost.

# Chapter 9

The path leading north was treacherous. Jagged cliffs rose on either side, and the wind howled through the narrow passes, carrying with it an eerie, almost sentient quality. Elias and Liora had been walking for hours, the cold biting through their cloaks as they pressed on toward the distant mountains where the ancient temple was rumored to lie.

The storm still loomed on the horizon, a swirling mass of darkness, but the skies above them were clear, for now. Elias could not help but feel like they were walking straight into the jaws of something monstrous.

As they climbed higher into the mountains, the terrain grew more hostile. The winds picked up, swirling around them like whispering voices, each gust seeming to carry a faint, indistinct murmur. At first, Elias thought it was just the sound of the wind cutting through the rocks, but as they moved deeper into the mountain pass, the whispers became more distinct—words, though still fragmented, drifted through the air.

"Can you hear that?" Elias asked, his hand instinctively moving to the hilt of his sword.

Liora nodded, her expression tight with concentration. "Yes. It is not the wind."

The words grew clearer, though still jumbled, as if spoken by many voices at once. *"Turn back... You cannot win... The shadows will consume you..."*

Elias's grip tightened on his sword. "What is this?"

# THE STORM OF SHADOWS

Liora's eyes darkened. "The mountain pass is known as the Winds of Memory. It is said that the voices of those who have died here, lost to the storm or to their own fears, remain. The wind carries their last thoughts, their final moments, forever repeating."

Elias shuddered, trying to block out the voices, but they pressed in, louder now. They seemed to echo in his mind, pulling at the corners of his consciousness, filling him with a growing sense of dread.

"*You will fail... There is no hope... The Harbinger cannot be stopped...*"

"Liora," Elias said, his voice strained. "How do we fight this?"

Liora stopped, her staff glowing faintly in the dim light. "We do not. The whispers cannot hurt us unless we let them. They are designed to feed off our fears, to make us doubt ourselves. The key is to ignore them. Focus on what is real—on each step forward. Do not give in."

Elias nodded, though the voices still clawed at his mind, trying to drag him into a spiral of doubt. He focused on the feel of the ground beneath his feet, the rhythm of his breathing, and the warmth of Liora's presence beside him. Slowly, the voices faded to a dull murmur, though they never disappeared entirely.

They pressed on, the wind still howling around them, but Elias felt a renewed determination. They were getting closer to the temple with each step, and though the mountain pass was dangerous, it was nothing compared to the battle they would soon face.

**An Unseen Threat**

Hours passed as they made their way deeper into the mountains. The path grew narrower, the cliffs steeper, until they were walking along a precarious ridge with sheer drops on either side. The whispers had grown faint, but the oppressive atmosphere remained, as if the mountain itself was watching them.

Elias scanned the cliffs above, his eyes narrowing. "Something's not right."

Liora glanced up, her brow furrowing. "What do you mean?"

Before Elias could respond, a low rumble echoed from above. He looked up just in time to see a massive boulder dislodge from the cliffside, tumbling toward them with terrifying speed.

"Move!" Elias shouted, grabbing Liora's arm and pulling her out of the way just as the boulder crashed into the path where they had been standing moments before, sending a shower of dust and debris into the air.

They stumbled back, breathing heavily as the ground shook beneath them. Elias coughed, wiping the dust from his face. "That wasn't an accident."

Liora nodded, her eyes scanning the cliffs above. "No. Something is here."

As if in response, a shadow flickered at the edge of Elias's vision. He turned, sword drawn, but there was nothing there—only the empty, windswept path behind them.

"We're being hunted," Liora said, her voice low.

Elias tightened his grip on his sword. "By what?"

Liora's gaze flickered to the cliffs above. "Something that doesn't want us to reach the temple."

The wind picked up again, carrying with it a deep, guttural growl that echoed through the mountains. Shadows danced at the edges of their vision, moving too quickly for Elias to track. Whatever it was, it was fast—too fast to see clearly.

Liora raised her staff, the light at its tip growing brighter as she prepared for a fight. "Stay close to me. Whatever it is, it is using the shadows to its advantage. We cannot let it separate us."

Elias nodded, stepping into position beside her. The growling grew louder, and the shadows began to swirl, taking shape, coalescing into figures—tall, hunched creatures with glowing eyes and elongated limbs, their bodies made of the same darkness that fueled the storm.

"They're not real," Liora said, her voice steady. "They are manifestations of the shadows, but they can still harm us. Be careful."

# THE STORM OF SHADOWS

The first creature lunged at them, its claws slicing through the air with terrifying speed. Elias barely had time to react, swinging his sword in a wide arc and cutting through the creature's form. It let out a piercing shriek as it dissolved into smoke, but more took its place.

"They just keep coming!" Elias shouted, cutting down another shadow creature as it leaped at him.

Liora's staff flared with light, sending a wave of energy through the air that scattered the nearest creatures, but it was clear they were outnumbered. The shadows swarmed around them, their forms shifting and multiplying as they attacked from all sides.

"We can't fight them all!" Elias called out, slashing through another creature as it lunged at him.

Liora's eyes narrowed in concentration. "We need to reach higher ground. The shadows are strongest here in the pass. If we can get above them, we will have the advantage."

Elias nodded, glancing up at the cliffs above. "There's a ledge up there—we can make it if we move fast."

Without waiting for a response, he grabbed Liora's hand and pulled her toward the base of the cliff. The shadow creatures hissed and shrieked as they pursued, but Elias did not look back. He focused on the path ahead, on the narrow ledge that offered a possible escape.

They scrambled up the rocky incline, the shadow creatures snapping at their heels. Elias's muscles burned with the effort, but he did not slow down. Not until they reached the ledge, just out of reach of the creatures below.

Panting, Elias turned to face the shadows. The creatures snarled and growled, but they did not follow them up the cliff. Instead, they lingered at the base, their glowing eyes fixed on Elias and Liora with predatory intensity.

"They can't reach us here," Liora said, her voice breathless but calm.

Elias nodded, wiping the sweat from his brow. "For now."

As they caught their breath, Elias stared down at the creatures below. The shadows writhed and twisted, their forms constantly shifting, as if they were part of the storm itself.

"They're not going to stop, are they?" Elias asked, his voice low.

Liora shook her head. "No. As long as we are in the mountains, they will keep coming. We must reach the temple before the storm catches up to us."

Elias looked out at the mountains ahead. The ancient temple was still far away, hidden deep within the jagged peaks, but they had no choice but to keep moving.

"Then let's go," Elias said, determination hardening his voice. "Before the shadows swallow us whole."

# Chapter 10

The temple loomed ahead, carved into the mountainside like a jagged wound. Its dark stone walls were slick with rain, the entrance framed by towering statues of forgotten gods, their faces worn smooth by time and weather. The swirling storm above had grown more intense, its dark clouds moving as if alive, churning with malevolent energy. Elias and Liora stood at the edge of the clearing, staring up at the colossal structure that housed the heart of the Harbinger's power.

"We've finally made it," Elias said, his voice tinged with awe and dread. He could feel the oppressive energy radiating from the temple, a dark pulse that set his teeth on edge.

Liora stepped forward, her violet eyes narrowing as she studied the ancient architecture. "The Temple of Dread. This is where it all began, where the first shadow was summoned into our world."

Elias tightened his grip on his sword. "And where it's going to end."

The air around them was thick with tension, the storm above crackling with dark magic. Every step they took toward the temple felt like walking into the jaws of some great beast, ready to devour them whole.

**The Threshold**

As they approached the temple's entrance, a sudden gust of wind howled through the mountains, carrying with it a voice—deep, cold, and echoing in the recesses of their minds.

*"You cannot stop what is already in motion. The storm will consume all."*

Elias stopped, his breath catching in his throat. The voice was not like the whispers they had heard in the pass; this was something older, darker, and infinitely more dangerous.

Liora's face was grim. "It is the Harbinger. It knows we are here."

Elias swallowed hard, his heart pounding in his chest. "So, what do we do?"

Liora lifted her staff, the gem at its tip glowing with a faint light. "We enter. The heart of its power lies within. If we can destroy it, we can weaken the Harbinger and end the storm."

The massive stone doors of the temple stood slightly ajar, as if inviting them in. A thick, cold mist seeped from the darkness beyond, curling around their ankles like fingers of shadow.

With a deep breath, Elias nodded. "Let's finish this."

Together, they stepped through the entrance and into the belly of the beast.

**The Descent**

The inside of the temple was vast, its walls carved with ancient runes that glowed faintly in the dim light. The floor was made of polished black stone, cold and slick beneath their boots. The sound of their footsteps echoed eerily through the massive halls, and the deeper they ventured, the more oppressive the atmosphere became.

Shadows clung to every corner, watching, waiting.

Elias felt a growing sense of unease as they descended deeper into the temple. The weight of the darkness pressed down on him, making it harder to breathe, harder to think. He could feel the Harbinger's presence, closer now, its power pulsing through the very stone of the temple.

Liora, ever calm, led the way, her staff lighting their path. But even she seemed to feel the weight of the shadows here. Her movements were slower, more deliberate, as if every step required effort.

"This place," Elias whispered, "it feels... alive."

# THE STORM OF SHADOWS

Liora nodded. "It is. The temple was built not just to house the heart of the Harbinger's power but to channel it. The shadows you see are part of the storm itself."

As they moved deeper, they came to a wide, open chamber. At its center stood a massive altar, and upon it, a glowing black stone—larger than any they had seen before. It pulsed with dark energy, its surface swirling with shadows. This was the heart of the storm, the source of the Harbinger's power.

"The Shadowheart," Liora whispered. "We destroy that, and we destroy the Harbinger."

**The Final Guardian**

Before they could take another step, a low rumble echoed through the chamber. The shadows on the walls began to shift, swirling together to form a massive figure—a guardian of the temple, forged from the darkness itself.

It was tall and monstrous, its body made of pure shadow, its eyes glowing a sickly green. It let out a deep, guttural growl as it stepped forward, blocking their path to the altar.

Elias raised his sword, his heart racing. "Guess it won't be that easy."

The creature lunged at them with surprising speed, its clawed hands reaching for Elias. He dodged to the side, narrowly avoiding the attack, and swung his sword at the creature. His blade passed through the shadowy form with little resistance, barely slowing it down.

"It's not solid!" Elias shouted. "How do we fight this thing?"

Liora stepped forward, her staff glowing brighter. "We cannot fight it like a normal enemy. It is made of pure shadow. We need to disrupt its form."

She raised her staff high, and with a word of power, a beam of light shot from the gem at its tip, striking the shadow creature in the chest. The creature shrieked, its form flickering and distorting as the light tore through it.

"Light!" Elias realized. "That's its weakness."

He moved quickly, dodging another swipe from the creature and positioning himself near one of the glowing runes carved into the walls. With a quick strike, he drove his sword into the rune, causing it to flare with bright light. The shadow creature recoiled, its form flickering again as the light weakened it.

Liora continued to channel her magic, sending beams of light at the creature, while Elias moved from rune to rune, activating each one to fill the chamber with light. The lighter they brought into the room, the weaker the creature became, its form breaking apart, piece by piece.

With one final, desperate roar, the creature lunged at Liora, but Elias was faster. He activated the last rune, flooding the chamber with blinding light. The creature let out a final, ear-piercing shriek before disintegrating into nothingness.

**The Heart of the Storm**

With the guardian defeated, the chamber fell silent, save for the faint pulsing of the Shadowheart on the altar.

Elias and Liora approached it cautiously, the dark stone radiating a palpable aura of malevolence. It was alive with the power of the storm, its surface swirling with darkness.

"This is it," Liora said softly. "The source of the Harbinger's power."

Elias gripped his sword tightly, staring down at the stone. "How do we destroy it?"

Liora's gaze hardened. "We need to sever its connection to the storm. If we strike it down with enough force, it will break the flow of magic, and the storm will lose its power."

Elias raised his sword, preparing for the strike, but before he could bring it down, the voice of the Harbinger echoed through the chamber once more.

*"You are fools. The storm cannot be stopped. Even if you destroy this vessel, I will return. The shadows are eternal."*

Elias hesitated, the weight of the Harbinger's words sinking in.

# THE STORM OF SHADOWS

Liora placed a hand on his arm, her voice steady. "Do not listen to it. The Harbinger wants you to doubt yourself. We must do this, Elias. For everyone."

With a deep breath, Elias nodded. He raised his sword high, channeling every ounce of strength he had left, and brought it down on the Shadowheart with a powerful strike.

The stone cracked, dark energy exploding outward in a wave of shadow and light. Elias and Liora were thrown back as the ground shook, the storm above roaring in response. But as the light cleared, the Shadowheart lay shattered on the altar, its dark energy dissipating into the air like smoke.

The chamber grew still. The oppressive weight of the darkness had lifted.

"It's done," Elias whispered, barely able to believe it.

Liora nodded, though her eyes were filled with both relief and caution. "The Harbinger is weakened, but not destroyed. The storm will take time to dissipate, but we have broken its hold."

Elias let out a breath he had not realized he had been holding. They had done it. The heart of the storm was no more.

The air in the temple had grown unnervingly still. Elias and Liora stood in the wake of their victory, the shattered remains of the Shadowheart littering the ancient altar. But the eerie silence that followed left little comfort. Outside, the swirling storm raged on, although it no longer felt as suffocating.

Elias rubbed his hand over his face, feeling the weight of exhaustion settle in. "We broke the heart, but the storm is still out there."

Liora's expression was tight with focus, her violet eyes scanning the shifting shadows along the temple walls. "The Harbinger's essence still lingers. It was weakened, but not vanquished. The storm is its anchor—it will continue to fight if even a shred of its power remains."

Elias nodded, still catching his breath. "So, what now?"

Liora stepped forward, her gaze landing on the remains of the Shadowheart. "Now, we sever the last thread. The storm's core may lie in the skies above, but its anchor to this world... it is here, beneath the temple."

Elias's brow furrowed. "Beneath?"

Liora knelt, her staff glowing faintly as she traced her fingers along the ancient stone of the temple floor. "The Shadowheart wasn't just a vessel—it was a key." The light from her staff flickered, revealing faint cracks in the stone, almost imperceptible. "There is a seal under this chamber. Something ancient... something that holds the Harbinger's true essence."

Elias felt a chill crawl up his spine. "Are you saying the Harbinger itself is buried here?"

Liora stood, her expression grim. "It was bound here long ago by ancient magic. The storm is a manifestation of its power, a way to break free. If we do not destroy its essence, it will keep coming back."

The air seemed to thrum with tension as the realization sank in. The battle they had fought was only a prelude to the true danger—the Harbinger had been using the storm to reclaim its power and rise once more.

"How do we get down there?" Elias asked, stepping closer to the center of the room.

Liora raised her staff, muttering an incantation under her breath. The runes carved into the floor glowed with a sickly green light as the stone beneath them trembled. Slowly, the floor cracked and crumbled away, revealing a spiral staircase descending into a dark abyss.

"Whatever lies below," Liora said, "we must face it. The Harbinger's prison is weakening, and it will throw everything it has at us to stop its final defeat."

Elias clenched his sword, steeling himself for what lay ahead. "Then let's finish this."

**The Descent into Darkness**

## THE STORM OF SHADOWS

The staircase wound downward into the earth, each step heavier than the last. The deeper they went, the colder the air became, thick with the stench of decay and rot. The walls around them were smooth, made of a strange black stone that seemed to drink in the light of Liora's staff, leaving only the faintest glow to guide their way.

As they descended, Elias felt a growing pressure in his chest, as if the air itself was pressing down on him, suffocating him. The presence of the Harbinger grew stronger, palpable in the dark, echoing passage.

"Can you feel it?" Elias asked, his voice strained.

Liora nodded, her grip tightening on her staff. "It is close. The prison was never meant to hold the Harbinger forever. The ancients knew it would eventually weaken, but they hoped to buy enough time."

"Time for what?"

"For someone like us to end it for good."

They reached the bottom of the staircase, stepping into a vast, circular chamber. The walls were lined with ancient, crumbling statues of faceless figures, their arms outstretched as if in supplication. At the center of the chamber, a massive stone sarcophagus lay, its surface etched with glowing runes. The air was thick with dark magic, swirling around the sarcophagus like a vortex.

"This is it," Liora whispered. "The Harbinger's true essence lies within."

Elias took a deep breath, his heart pounding in his chest. "How do we destroy it?"

Liora's face was pale but determined. "We must sever its connection to the world completely. That means breaking the rules that bind its prison and releasing its essence. Then, we can destroy it."

Elias swallowed hard. "Sounds easy enough."

But before they could take another step, the air around them seemed to shimmer, and from the shadows, the figure of the Harbinger began to materialize.

It was no longer the storm of darkness they had fought before, but a twisted, towering form of pure malevolence, its body wreathed in shadow and lightning. Its eyes burned with a cold, otherworldly light, and its voice rumbled through the chamber like thunder.

*"You are too late, mortals."*

Elias felt a wave of pure fear crash over him as the Harbinger's presence filled the chamber. Its power was overwhelming, suffocating, and for a moment, he doubted they could win.

Liora's voice broke through the haze of dread. "Elias, focus! We must break the runes—now!"

Elias snapped out of his fear, nodding quickly as he rushed toward the sarcophagus. Liora raised her staff, unleashing a blast of magic at the Harbinger to keep it at bay, but the dark entity barely flinched, stepping forward with a slow, deliberate malice.

With every step the Harbinger took, the ground shook, and the air became heavier, the shadows around them growing more restless.

*"You cannot destroy me,"* the Harbinger growled. *"I am eternal. Darkness cannot be killed—it can only be delayed."*

Elias gritted his teeth, slamming his sword into the first rune carved into the sarcophagus. The stone cracked, and the air trembled as the binding spell weakened. The Harbinger let out an enraged roar, lashing out with tendrils of shadow that coiled toward Elias.

Liora stepped in front of him, her staff glowing brightly as she formed a barrier of light to block the attack. "Hurry!" she shouted, straining under the pressure of the Harbinger's assault.

Elias moved quickly, striking at the remaining runes, each one causing the dark energy in the room to fluctuate violently. The Harbinger howled in fury, its form growing more erratic as the bindings holding it in place weakened.

Finally, with one last strike, the final rune shattered, and the sarcophagus began to crumble. The Harbinger let out a deafening

# THE STORM OF SHADOWS

scream as its prison collapsed, and the dark energy it had been gathering for centuries began to spill out into the chamber.

But instead of fleeing, the Harbinger surged forward, its essence coiling toward Elias and Liora with terrifying speed.

*"You cannot win!"* it roared. *"I will consume you both!"*

Liora raised her staff, her voice rising above the chaos. "Elias! Now!"

With no time to think, Elias plunged his sword into the heart of the dark energy swirling from the sarcophagus. The blade glowed with a blinding light as it connected with the Harbinger's essence, sending shockwaves through the chamber. The air screamed with the sound of clashing forces, light against shadow, as the Harbinger's form writhed in agony.

The shadows around them shattered like glass, and the Harbinger's form began to disintegrate, its essence pulled apart by the power of Elias's strike.

*"No... this cannot be..."* the Harbinger's voice faded into a whisper; its final words lost to the void as its essence was obliterated.

The storm of shadows was no more.

**The Aftermath**

The chamber was still once again, the oppressive weight of the Harbinger's presence finally gone. Elias stood in silence, breathing heavily as the reality of what they had just accomplished settled in. Liora lowered her staff, her body trembling with exhaustion.

"It's over," Elias whispered, his voice filled with disbelief.

Liora nodded, though her eyes remained fixed on the now-empty sarcophagus. "For now."

The storm outside had begun to clear, the dark clouds dispersing and letting rays of sunlight breakthrough for the first time in what felt like an eternity.

Elias turned to Liora, a small, weary smile on his face. "We did it."

Liora met his gaze, her expression softening as she smiled back. "Yes. But the darkness will always be out there, waiting for its chance. We must be ready."

Elias nodded, understanding the weight of her words. The Harbinger had been defeated, but the world would never be free of shadows. They could only push them back—for a time.

Together, they climbed the stairs, leaving the shattered remains of the Harbinger's prison behind. The storm was gone, but the world they had fought to save was forever changed.

And so were they.

# Chapter 11

The temple's entrance felt surreal as Elias and Liora emerged from the depths. The sky, once heavy with dark clouds, now stretched open above them, bathed in the soft hues of a fading storm. Rays of sunlight pierced the gray clouds, shining down like beacons of hope. But as beautiful as it was, the silence that followed the battle was thick with a strange unease.

Elias paused, his body still aching from the strain of their confrontation below. He glanced at Liora, whose face bore the same quiet reflection.

"We won," Elias said softly, more to himself than to her. His voice sounded distant in the open air, as if the temple's shadows had followed them out.

Liora's violet eyes, so often sharp and calculating, were clouded with a different emotion now—one that Elias could not quite name. She nodded, though her expression remained guarded.

"Yes," she said, her voice softer than before. "But the echoes of the storm still remain."

Elias frowned, turning to the horizon. In the distance, where the storm had raged the fiercest, the land was scarred. The fields they once knew were left torn apart by the relentless winds, and the sky still shimmered with faint traces of dark energy. Though the Harbinger had been defeated, its presence lingered, like a shadow that refused to fade completely.

**A World Reborn**

They began their descent from the temple, following the winding path back to the villages they had left behind. As they walked, the silence between them deepened. Elias could feel the weight of what they had done—and what remained undone. The Harbinger was gone, but the damage it had wrought was far from over.

As they approached the outskirts of the first village, a haunting scene awaited them. Homes lay in ruins, toppled trees and broken stone marking the path of the storm. The villagers who had survived looked up as they passed, their faces hollow with exhaustion and loss.

A young girl, no older than ten, stood near a fallen tree, her eyes wide and distant. Elias's heart clenched at the sight of her. He recognized that look—one he had worn many times in his own life. It was the look of someone who had seen too much, too soon.

Liora stopped beside the girl, kneeling. "Are you hurt?" she asked gently.

The girl shook her head, but she did not speak. Her gaze remained fixed on the horizon, where the remnants of the storm still lingered.

"She's not alone," Elias murmured, scanning the village. There were others—many others—just like her. Survivors of the storm, but forever marked by it.

The reality of their victory settled over him like a weight. They had saved the world from the Harbinger, but they had not been able to save everyone.

**The Weight of Leadership**

As they moved deeper into the village, the remaining elders gathered around them. Faces lined with age and worry, they approached cautiously, as if unsure whether to celebrate or mourn.

An older man with a cane stepped forward, his eyes filled with both gratitude and grief. "The storm has passed, but it has left us broken," he said, his voice shaking. "What remains for us now?"

Elias glanced at Liora, who remained quiet, her expression unreadable. He knew that she, too, was wrestling with the enormity of what they had done—and what still lay ahead.

# THE STORM OF SHADOWS

Elias spoke, his voice steady but heavy with responsibility. "We stopped the Harbinger, but the storm's effects will linger. The land is scarred, and the darkness may return. But you have survived, and together, you can rebuild."

The elder nodded, though his expression remained somber. "Rebuild, yes, but it will take time—and many of us have nothing left."

Liora finally spoke, her voice soft but clear. "The Harbinger's power was great, but it drew on fear and despair. The fact that you are standing here now means you have already won the first battle. The rest will be difficult, but the storm's shadow does not have to define the future."

The villagers listened, and though their faces remained etched with sorrow, there was a flicker of hope in their eyes.

**New Beginnings**

As the days passed, Elias and Liora stayed in the village, helping where they could. Rebuilding homes, tending to the wounded, and reassuring the shaken. Elias often found himself wandering through the ruins, reflecting on the path that had brought them here. He had spent so long fighting against the storm, against the shadows, that now, with it gone, he was not sure what to do next.

Liora seemed to sense this, and one evening, as they sat around a small fire, she spoke quietly.

"We've won the battle, but the war... it never truly ends."

Elias looked at her, his brow furrowing. "You mean the Harbinger?"

She shook her head. "Not just the Harbinger. Darkness will always find a way. Whether it is in the form of an ancient being or the fear in people's hearts, it will always be there, waiting."

Elias sighed, leaning back against the log behind him. "So, what are we supposed to do now? Keep fighting? Keep chasing shadows?"

Liora smiled faintly, though there was a hint of sadness in her eyes. "We do not have to chase the shadows. We just must make sure they do not swallow us whole."

Her words lingered in the cool night air, and for a long moment, they sat in silence, watching the flames dance in the fire.

**A Farewell**

When the time finally came for them to leave the village, it felt bittersweet. The villagers had begun the process of rebuilding, their spirits slowly lifting as the days went on. The scars of the storm were still visible, but hope had taken root once more.

As they prepared to depart, the elder approached them again, his cane tapping against the stone path.

"We owe you both a great debt," he said, his voice filled with gratitude. "Without you, there would be no village left to rebuild."

Elias shook his head. "You do not owe us anything. We did what we had to."

Liora stepped forward, her gaze soft but serious. "Take care of yourselves. The world is still fragile, and there may be more trials ahead."

The elder nodded, his eyes gleaming with understanding. "We will."

With that, Elias and Liora turned and began their journey, leaving the village behind. The storm had passed, but the world ahead of them was still uncertain.

As they walked, Elias found himself wondering what the future would hold. Would the darkness return? Would they ever truly be free of the shadows?

Liora's words echoed in his mind: *We do not have to chase the shadows. We just must make sure they do not swallow us whole.*

And with that, Elias understood. The battles would continue, but so would the light. And if there was light, there would always be hope.

# Chapter 12

The sun had barely risen when Elias and Liora set out from the village, the air still cools with the remnants of the night. They had been walking for hours, and the weight of their recent victory pressed heavily on their shoulders. Yet, something stirred in the distance, something Elias could not quite put into words. The storm was gone, but the air itself felt charged—like the world was holding its breath.

Liora paused, her eyes narrowing as she scanned the horizon. "Do you feel that?"

Elias frowned. "Feel what?"

Liora's gaze sharpened, her body tense. "Something's coming."

Before Elias could respond, a low rumble shook the ground beneath their feet. He spun around, eyes wide, searching for the source. The earth quaked again, this time with more force, sending a flock of birds screeching into the air.

A crack ripped through the ground a few feet away, the soil splitting open as a jagged tear raced across the landscape.

"What the—" Elias did not have time to finish his sentence before a deafening roar echoed through the sky, and a massive figure burst from the earth, shrouded in shadow and flame.

Elias's heart stopped. He recognized it instantly.

"No," he whispered, his grip tightening on his sword. "It can't be."

**The Harbinger Reborn**

The colossal creature rose from the ground, its form wreathed in black fire. Dark wings unfurled from its back, sending gusts of hot wind blasting across the field. The Harbinger, or at least, what remained of it, had returned. Its eyes burned with an unnatural light, no longer the pure shadow of before, but something darker, something angrier. The essence of the storm had merged with something else—something older.

Elias and Liora took a step back as the Harbinger let out another ear-splitting roar, its gaze locking onto them.

"Impossible," Liora breathed, her voice tight with disbelief. "We destroyed it. This... this should not be possible!"

The ground trembled again, and with terrifying speed, the Harbinger lunged forward, its claws tearing through the earth as it surged toward them.

Elias barely had time to raise his sword before the creature was upon them. He ducked under a swipe from its massive claws, rolling to the side as Liora summoned a barrier of light to block the next attack.

"We need a plan!" Elias shouted, trying to catch his breath as the Harbinger's claws slammed into Liora's barrier, sending cracks rippling through the protective shield.

Liora's voice was strained as she held the barrier in place. "It is not just the Harbinger anymore—its power has grown. There is something else fueling it!"

Elias's mind raced as he dodged another strike, the ground beneath him exploding into fragments. This was not the same enemy they had faced before. The Harbinger's new form was more powerful, more relentless. If they did not act fast, they would not survive.

# THE STORM OF SHADOWS

**The Sky Burns**

Suddenly, the air around them shifted again, but this time, it was not from the Harbinger. The sky above began to darken, swirling clouds forming out of nowhere. Lightning crackled across the sky, and the temperature dropped sharply.

A storm was brewing—but not like the one before. This storm felt different. More primal. More deadly.

Liora's eyes widened as she looked up. "The storm... it is connected to it. It is drawing power from the sky itself."

Elias cursed under his breath, dodging another swipe from the Harbinger. "Great. We took out one storm only to face another!"

With the storm gaining strength overhead, the Harbinger became even more aggressive. Its attacks came faster, its claws slashing through the air with deadly precision. Elias barely managed to block a strike, the force of it sending him skidding backward.

Liora raised her staff, channeling energy into a powerful spell. "We need to sever the connection! If we do not, the storm will keep fueling it until it is unstoppable!"

Elias nodded, his grip on his sword tightening. "Right. How do we do that?"

Liora's eyes flashed with determination. "The heart of the storm—it is in the sky. We need to disrupt the core, or we will be overwhelmed."

Another deafening roar echoed from the Harbinger as it lunged toward them once more. Elias jumped to the side, his sword flashing as he struck at one of its wings, sparks flying as his blade connected with the creature's hardened scales.

"Go!" Elias shouted. "I'll hold it off—disrupt the core!"

Liora hesitated for a split second, her gaze flicking between Elias and the storm overhead. She nodded, raising her staff high as she began to chant. The wind whipped around her, swirling with the growing power of her spell. Lightning arced through the air, drawn toward her as she summoned energy from the storm itself.

The Harbinger snarled, its attention shifting toward Liora as it sensed her gathering power. It lunged forward, but Elias was faster. He threw himself in front of Liora, blocking the creature's path.

"Not so fast!" Elias shouted, driving his sword into the ground and sending a shockwave of energy through the earth. The ground beneath the Harbinger trembled, throwing the massive creature off balance for a moment.

It was not much, but it was enough.

**The Heart of the Storm**

Liora's chant reached its peak, her staff glowing with a blinding light. With a fierce cry, she thrust the staff upward, releasing the energy she had gathered. The sky split open as a massive bolt of lightning shot downward, striking the core of the storm.

The effect was immediate.

The storm overhead shuddered, its swirling clouds faltering as the connection between the Harbinger and the storm began to fray. The creature let out a furious roar, its form flickering as the power fueling it was disrupted.

Elias did not waste a second. He charged forward, his sword gleaming with the light of Liora's spell. With a powerful swing, he struck the Harbinger's chest, driving his blade deep into its core.

The creature screamed, a sound so full of rage and pain that it shook the very earth beneath them. Dark energy erupted from the wound, swirling around the Harbinger like a vortex.

"Now!" Liora shouted, her voice cutting through the chaos.

Elias summoned all his strength, pushing his blade deeper into the creature's chest. The Harbinger's form began to disintegrate, its body unraveling as the storm's power was stripped away.

With a final, earth-shattering scream, the Harbinger exploded into a burst of dark energy, scattering into the wind.

# THE STORM OF SHADOWS

## A Calm After the Chaos

The storm overhead vanished as quickly as it had appeared. The clouds dissipated, the sky returning to its natural blue, and the earth around them grew still.

Elias stood in silence, panting heavily, his sword still glowing faintly from the power of the battle. Liora approached him slowly, her face pale but determined.

"Is it... over?" Elias asked, his voice barely a whisper.

Liora nodded, though her eyes were wary. "For now."

They stood in the aftermath, surrounded by the broken earth and the fading remnants of the Harbinger's power. But even as the world returned to calm, Elias could not shake the feeling that something still lingered in the air—something darker, waiting in the shadows.

The storm had passed, but the echoes of its fury were far from gone.

# Chapter 13

The sky, once a battlefield of lightning and fury, was now a serene canvas of blues and whites. Yet, as the last remnants of the Harbinger's dark energy dissipated into the wind, a chilling silence fell over the land. Elias and Liora stood side by side, their hearts still racing from the battle they had just survived. But victory, though hard-earned, felt incomplete.

Elias wiped sweat from his brow, his hand trembling slightly as he sheathed his sword. "We destroyed it again," he muttered, eyes scanning the horizon, "but why doesn't it feel like it's over?"

Liora, her face still pales from the exertion of summoning the storm's core, shook her head. "Because something is wrong. The storm's power... it was more than just the Harbinger. There was something else—another presence feeding it."

Elias's stomach twisted. "You think there is more out there? Something bigger than the Harbinger?"

Liora did not answer immediately. Instead, she knelt and placed a hand on the scorched earth where the Harbinger had fallen. A faint, dark mist still clung to the ground, as if reluctant to vanish completely. She closed her eyes, her fingers tracing the edges of the energy.

"There's something ancient here," she whispered. "Older than the Harbinger, older than the storm. Something watching."

**The Watcher in the Shadows**

Elias felt a shiver crawl up his spine. He took a step closer to Liora, his hand resting on the hilt of his sword. "Watching? You mean something has been controlling it this whole time?"

# THE STORM OF SHADOWS

Liora stood slowly, her violet eyes now filled with a deep concern. "I do not know if 'controlling' is the right word. But it was guiding the storm, pushing the Harbinger toward us. It feels... intentional."

A gust of wind blew across the landscape, and for a moment, it felt as if the world itself was holding its breath, listening.

"We need answers," Elias said, his voice firm. "We cannot keep facing this without knowing what we are up against. If there is something bigger out there, we need to find it."

Liora nodded, her expression grim. "Agreed. But where do we start?"

Just as the question left her lips, the ground beneath their feet trembled again. But this time, it was not the violent quake of the Harbinger's return. It was a softer vibration, like the pulsing heartbeat of something buried deep within the earth.

Elias and Liora exchanged a glance.

"The temple," Liora said, her voice barely above a whisper. "There's something below it."

Without another word, they turned and made their way back toward the ancient temple they had left behind. The structure loomed in the distance, its dark stone walls standing defiant against the sky. But as they drew closer, something strange began to happen. The temple, once silent and lifeless, now hummed with an eerie energy. Shadows flickered along its walls, and faint whispers, barely audible, seemed to echo from within.

**Beneath the Temple**

As they entered the temple once more, the air inside was thick with a suffocating darkness. The familiar corridors felt different now—alive with a presence that neither of them could fully comprehend. The torches lining the walls flickered wildly, casting long, twisted shadows that danced across the stone.

Liora gripped her staff tightly, her eyes scanning the shifting shadows. "Whatever is down here, it's waking up."

Elias nodded, his hand hovering over his sword as they descended deeper into the temple. They had explored this place before, but something had changed since their last visit. The walls seemed to pulse with dark energy, as though the temple itself was alive, responding to their presence.

As they reached the lower levels, they came to a massive stone door, intricately carved with symbols neither of them recognized. Dark tendrils of energy seeped from the cracks in the door, swirling like smoke in the air.

"This wasn't here before," Elias said, his voice tense.

Liora stepped forward, her hand hovering over the symbols. "It is a seal. A powerful one. Whatever is behind this door... it has been locked away for centuries."

Elias felt the hairs on the back of his neck stand up. "Do we really want to open it?"

Liora hesitated, but then nodded. "If we are going to understand what is happening, we need to see what is inside. We need to face it."

Elias swallowed hard, drawing his sword as Liora began chanting under her breath. The symbols on the door glowed faintly, and the stone began to shift, grinding slowly as the seal was broken.

With a deep, echoing groan, the door swung open, revealing a dark chamber beyond. The air inside was thick, oppressive, as if centuries of darkness had been locked away in this room. But more unsettling than the darkness was the massive stone pedestal at the center of the chamber.

And atop it, a pulsating, black orb of energy.

**The Heart of Shadows**

Liora's breath caught in her throat. "That... that is it. The source of the storm. The power that was feeding the Harbinger."

Elias stared at the orb, his instincts screaming at him to leave, to shut the door and walk away. But he knew they could not. This was

# THE STORM OF SHADOWS

what had been driving the storm, what had fueled the Harbinger's return. If they did not stop it now, it would only continue to grow.

As they stepped into the chamber, the orb seemed to react, its surface rippling like water disturbed by a stone. The whispers they had heard before grew louder, filling the room with a chorus of voices—some speaking in languages they could not understand, others in low, guttural tones that chilled them to the bone.

"This is ancient magic," Liora said, her voice barely above a whisper. "Older than anything I've ever encountered."

Elias raised his sword, pointing it toward the orb. "Can we destroy it?"

Liora hesitated. "I do not know. But we cannot leave it here."

Before they could act, the orb pulsed violently, and from its surface, tendrils of dark energy shot out, wrapping around them like chains. Elias slashed at the tendrils with his sword, but they were too fast, too strong. The dark energy pulled them toward the orb, tightening around their bodies like a vice.

Liora gasped, her hands glowing with light as she tried to summon a spell to break free. But the orb's power was overwhelming, its whispers growing louder, more insistent.

"Elias!" she shouted, her voice filled with panic. "It's trying to pull us in!"

Elias struggled against the tendrils, his muscles straining as he fought to free himself. But the more they struggled, the stronger the orb's pull became.

Amid the chaos, a single voice rose above the others—a voice that chilled Elias to his core.

"You've come far," the voice hissed, its tone dripping with malice. "But you cannot stop what is already in motion. The storm was only the beginning. The true darkness is yet to come."

Elias's heart pounded in his chest. "Who are you?!"

The voice chuckled darkly. "I am the shadow behind the storm. I am the one who watches. And soon, I will be the one who *rules*."

With a final, violent pulse, the orb's tendrils tightened, dragging Elias and Liora toward its dark heart.

And then—everything went black.

# Chapter 14

Darkness consumed Elias and Liora as they were dragged into the heart of the orb. The sensation of falling was overwhelming, as though the ground had vanished beneath them and they were plunging into an endless void. Elias could not see, could not breathe—just the crushing weight of nothingness pressing in from every side. The whispers, louder now, swirled around them, mocking, jeering, growing ever more sinister.

Then, just as abruptly as the descent began, the fall stopped. Elias gasped as his feet hit solid ground, though he could see nothing. A heavy mist clung to the air, and for a moment, all was silent.

"Liora?" Elias called out, his voice echoing in the void.

A faint glow flickered in the distance, and then Liora's voice pierced the darkness. "I'm here!"

Elias followed the light, his heart racing. As he approached, Liora came into view, her staff glowing softly in the dark, illuminating a small circle around them. She looked shaken but unharmed.

"Where are we?" Elias asked, glancing around. The mist curled in every direction, obscuring any sense of where they were or how far they had fallen.

"I don't know," Liora whispered, her eyes wide as she scanned the shadows. "This place... it feels wrong. Like we have been pulled into another realm."

Elias nodded, his grip tightening on his sword. "Whatever it is, we need to find a way out."

**The Realm of Shadows**

As they cautiously moved through the mist, the landscape around them slowly began to take shape. Jagged rocks jutted up from the ground, their surfaces slick with dark energy. The sky—or what passed for a sky—was a swirling vortex of black and violet, streaked with occasional flashes of lightning. The air itself felt thick, heavy with a dark presence.

"We're not in the temple anymore," Elias muttered, his eyes scanning the unfamiliar surroundings. "This place... it's alive with dark magic."

Liora nodded, her expression tense. "We've crossed into the Shadow Realm."

Elias looked at her sharply. "The Shadow Realm? I thought that was just a myth."

Liora shook her head, her voice grave. "It is real. A dimension beyond our own, where darkness reigns and the most ancient, malevolent forces are sealed away. The Harbinger must have been connected to this place, but it is much worse than I imagined."

Elias felt a chill crawl up his spine. "Then the voice we heard—"

"—belongs to something that has existed long before the Harbinger," Liora finished. "Something that's been waiting for this moment."

A low rumble echoed through the mist, and Elias raised his sword instinctively. Shadows shifted in the distance, moving with a life of their own, watching them.

"Whatever it is," Elias said, his voice low, "it knows we're here."

**The Watcher's Lair**

After what felt like hours of walking through the twisted landscape, Elias and Liora came to a massive stone structure rising from the ground. Its jagged spires reached toward the stormy sky, and dark energy pulsed from its core. At the top of the structure was an enormous black gate, inscribed with ancient runes that glowed faintly in the gloom.

# THE STORM OF SHADOWS

"This is it," Liora whispered. "The source of the power we felt. The heart of the storm."

Elias stared at the gate, his pulse quickening. "Are we ready for this? We do not even know what is behind that door."

Liora's eyes hardened. "We do not have a choice. Whatever is controlling the storms, whatever pulled us into this realm—it is here. If we do not stop it, it will consume our world."

Taking a deep breath, Elias nodded. Together, they approached the gate. As they got closer, the air around them grew heavier, the whispers louder, more insistent.

Liora raised her staff, and the runes on the gate flared to life, casting an eerie glow over the stone. With a deep, resonating groan, the gate slowly creaked open, revealing a vast chamber beyond.

Inside, the chamber was enormous, its walls lined with flickering shadows. At the center of the room, perched atop a throne of twisted black stone, sat a figure cloaked in darkness. Its form was barely visible, wrapped in the shadows like a living nightmare.

"Welcome," the figure hissed, its voice dripping with malice. "You've done well to make it this far."

Elias tightened his grip on his sword, his eyes narrowing. "Who are you?"

The figure chuckled, the sound reverberating through the chamber. "I am the one who has watched from the darkness for eons. I am the one who set the storm in motion. And now, I am the one who will take what is mine."

Liora stepped forward, her staff glowing with light. "You're behind the storm, the Harbinger, everything."

The figure tilted its head, the shadows shifting around it like tendrils. "The Harbinger was but a tool—a means to an end. It paved the way for my return, but its purpose is done. Now, I will claim this realm... and yours."

Elias stepped forward; his sword gleaming. "Not if we stop you."

The figure rose from the throne, its dark form towering over them. "You think you can defeat me? Foolish mortals. I am the darkness that has existed since the dawn of time. You are nothing but fleeting sparks, soon to be snuffed out."

## The Final Confrontation

Without warning, the figure lashed out, its shadowy form expanding, filling the chamber with dark energy. Elias barely managed to raise his sword in time to block the first strike, the force of it sending him stumbling backward. Liora raised her staff, summoning a barrier of light that held the shadows at bay, but the figure's power was immense, far greater than anything they had faced before.

"Liora!" Elias shouted, struggling to his feet. "We need to combine our power!"

Liora nodded, her face grim. "We need to weaken it first. Its connection to the storm is its strength—if we sever that, we can defeat it."

As the figure's shadowy tendrils lashed out again, Elias and Liora split, dodging the attacks as they circled around the chamber. The figure's laughter echoed through the room, dark and mocking.

"You think you can stop me?" it taunted, its voice filling the air. "I am the storm. I am the darkness."

Elias gritted his teeth, his mind racing. He could feel the dark energy pressing in on them, but he refused to back down. As the figure loomed above them, its shadowy form expanding, Elias saw an opening—a crack in the swirling storm of shadows surrounding it.

"Now!" he shouted, raising his sword high. Liora responded immediately, channeling all her energy into a single, blinding beam of light. The light struck the figure, and for a moment, the shadows around it faltered.

Elias did not hesitate. He charged forward, driving his sword into the heart of the darkness, piercing the very core of the figure's power.

# THE STORM OF SHADOWS

The figure let out a deafening roar, the sound shaking the chamber as the shadows writhed in agony. Dark energy exploded outward, but Liora's barrier held firm, shielding them from the blast.

For a moment, everything was still.

Then, slowly, the figure collapsed, its form dissolving into nothingness. The dark energy that had filled the chamber dissipated, and the oppressive weight lifted from the air.

### A Fragile Victory

Elias stood panting, his sword still glowing faintly from the battle. Liora lowered her staff, her face pale but determined.

"Is it over?" Elias asked, his voice hoarse.

Liora looked around the chamber, her eyes narrowing. "For now. But the storm... the power behind it is ancient. We may have defeated this creature, but the darkness it comes from still exists."

Elias nodded, his heart heavy with the weight of their fragile victory. "Then we'll be ready for whatever comes next."

As they made their way out of the chamber, the gate behind them slowly closing, the mist began to lift, and the path ahead became clear. But even as they stepped into the light, Elias could not shake the feeling that the true storm was still on the horizon, waiting for its moment to strike.

And when it did, they would have to face it again.

# Chapter 15

The climb back to the surface felt like an eternity, though the oppressive darkness of the Shadow Realm had dissipated. Every step weighed heavy on Elias and Liora, the recent battle still fresh in their minds. The air grew clearer, and the mist thinned, but there was no sense of victory, only an unsettling quiet.

At last, they emerged from the temple's depths into the open sky. The storm clouds that had once dominated the horizon were gone, leaving behind a clear, eerily serene day. The landscape seemed almost peaceful compared to the chaos of the battle below. Yet, beneath the stillness, an unspoken tension lingered.

Elias sheathed his sword, glancing around as if expecting the shadows to return at any moment. "It feels too quiet. Like we have missed something."

Liora stood beside him, her violet eyes scanning the horizon. "We have weakened the darkness, but the storm's source was not just the creature we defeated. There is something bigger at play."

Elias frowned. "The voice we heard—it wasn't just from that creature, was it?"

Liora nodded gravely. "No. That was a fragment of a much older, more powerful force. We only faced one manifestation of it. The real danger... it is still out there."

Elias's grip tightened around his sword hilt. "Then we need to find it before it finds us."

**A World on Edge**

As they made their way back to the nearby village, the devastation left by the storm was clear. Buildings lay in ruins, and the fields were still flooded from the relentless rain. Villagers, though alive, wandered aimlessly, their faces marked by fear and uncertainty.

Elias and Liora were greeted with quiet, haunted stares. No one spoke as they passed, but the weight of their gaze was heavy. These people had been through a nightmare, and while the storm had passed, the scars remained.

"The storm may be gone, but the fear lingers," Elias muttered, more to himself than to Liora.

Liora nodded. "People can sense when a battle is not truly over. They can feel the darkness beneath the surface."

They approached the village elder, a woman named Isolde, who had led the people to shelter during the storm. Her lined face was pale and weary, but her eyes held a quiet strength.

"You've returned," Isolde said, her voice rough. "The storm has passed. What did you find?"

Elias exchanged a glance with Liora before answering. "We destroyed the creature that fueled the storm, but we believe there is a greater force behind it—something older, darker. This is not over."

Isolde's expression did not falter, but her hands trembled slightly as she clasped them together. "I feared as much. I have lived long enough to know when a storm has more to it than wind and rain."

She sighed deeply, her gaze turning toward the distant horizon. "The storm may be gone for now, but something stirs in the shadows. I can feel it."

Liora stepped forward, her voice calm but firm. "We are going to continue our search. We need to understand what we are truly up against. But the village will need to prepare. If the darkness returns, you need to be ready."

Isolde nodded slowly. "We will do what we can. But I pray you find answers soon."

# THE STORM OF SHADOWS

## THE SEARCH FOR ANSWERS

As they left the village behind, Elias and Liora made their way through the ruined landscape, their thoughts heavy with unanswered questions. The battle they had fought felt like a mere prelude to something far worse, and neither of them could shake the feeling that they had only scratched the surface of the true threat.

"What do you think it is?" Elias asked as they walked, his voice quiet.

Liora shook her head. "I do not know. But whatever it is, it is ancient. Older than any magic I have encountered. The Shadow Realm is only one layer of its power. If it can manipulate storms, control creatures like the Harbinger, then its influence could be much wider."

Elias grunted. "Wider how? Are we talking about another storm, or something bigger?"

Liora's brow furrowed. "I do not think it is just about storms. The storms were a symptom, not the cause. This force—whatever it is—wants something. It is trying to break through into our world. And if it succeeds..."

She trailed off, but the implication was clear. If the darkness broke free, the devastation they had seen would only be the beginning.

They pressed on, making their way toward the distant mountains where rumors spoke of a forgotten library—an ancient stronghold of knowledge that might hold the answers they sought. The journey would be dangerous, but it was their only lead.

**Whispers in the Wind**

As they camped that night, the air grew colder, the winds picking up. Elias sat by the fire; his gaze fixed on the flickering flames. He could not shake the feeling that something was watching them. Ever since they left the temple, that oppressive presence had been lingering just out of reach, as if the shadows themselves were following their every step.

Liora sat across from him, her staff resting beside her. "You feel it too, don't you?"

Elias nodded. "Like we're being hunted."

Liora stared into the fire. "The darkness is not done with us. It may have retreated for now, but it is waiting. It is watching."

Suddenly, a gust of wind whipped through the camp, scattering the embers of the fire. Elias jumped to his feet, sword in hand, as the shadows around them seemed to ripple and shift.

"Liora—"

Before he could finish, the shadows coalesced into a dark figure, its form twisted and flickering like smoke. The same voice they had heard in the temple whispered from the darkness, its tone dripping with malice.

"You think you've escaped me?" the voice hissed. "You think you can hide?"

Elias's heart pounded in his chest. "What are you?"

The figure's eyes glowed faintly in the darkness, two pinpricks of red light. "I am the storm. I am the shadow. And I will not be denied."

With a sudden burst of speed, the figure lunged toward them, its shadowy tendrils reaching out to ensnare them. Elias slashed with his sword, but his blade passed through the figure like it was made of smoke.

Liora raised her staff, summoning a barrier of light to hold the figure at bay. "Elias, we need to run!"

Without hesitation, they turned and fled, the figure's laughter echoing behind them. The wind howled, and the shadows seemed to stretch and warp, twisting the landscape around them. But they ran, never looking back, knowing that the darkness was still chasing them. Elias and Liora sprinted through the twisting forest, the shadows stretching behind them like grasping hands. Every step felt heavier, as if the very air thickened with dark energy. The laughter of the shadowy figure echoed, following them like a predator closing in on its prey.

# THE STORM OF SHADOWS

"Faster!" Liora urged, her voice strained, her staff glowing faintly in her grip.

Branches scratched at their faces, and the wind howled louder, pushing against them with unnatural force. It was as if the very storm they had escaped was being summoned back, a dark reminder that their battle was not over. Elias could hear his heartbeat in his ears, each breath coming in ragged gasps. The figure's presence was like a weight on his back, pulling him into the abyss.

Suddenly, they burst through the tree line and found themselves at the edge of a ravine. The ground dropped sharply into a rocky chasm, the roaring sound of a river far below. Elias skidded to a stop, nearly toppling over the edge.

"No!" he shouted, turning around to face the darkness that was rapidly closing in. They were trapped.

Liora stood beside him, her staff glowing brighter now. She planted her feet firmly, eyes locked on the swirling shadows. "We make our stand here."

The shadowy figure emerged from the trees; its red eyes gleaming with malice. Its form flickered and twisted, as if it were both part of the world and separate from it. The wind howled, carrying its voice like a venomous whisper.

"You can't run forever," it hissed, its dark tendrils snaking across the ground toward them. "You are nothing against the storm. You will be consumed."

Elias raised his sword, his stance steady despite the terror coursing through him. "We're not running."

**A Desperate Fight**

The figure lunged, its tendrils whipping through the air with a sound like crackling thunder. Elias swung his sword, slicing through the darkness, but the tendrils reformed almost instantly, wrapping around his legs, pulling him toward the figure's swirling mass.

Liora reacted quickly, slamming her staff into the ground. A wave of light exploded outward, cutting through the tendrils, and forcing the shadowy figure to recoil. The light pulsed around them, holding the darkness at bay, but Liora's face was pale, her energy draining rapidly.

"I can't hold it off for long," she muttered, her voice strained. "We need a plan."

Elias struggled to his feet, the weight of the shadow's power pressing down on him. He glanced around, desperate for something—anything—that could give them an advantage. The ravine behind them was deep and treacherous, but the figure seemed hesitant to cross the barrier of light. It was not invincible, not yet.

"What if we could force it into the ravine?" Elias suggested, eyes darting between the shadow and the cliff's edge. "It is made of darkness, but it still has a form. If we can push it over, maybe the fall will weaken it."

Liora's brow furrowed as she considered the plan, her grip tightening on her staff. "It is risky. If it grabs one of us before it falls…"

Elias met her gaze, determination blazing in his eyes. "It's a risk we have to take."

The shadowy figure reformed, its red eyes narrowing as it gathered itself for another strike. This time, it was more cautious, watching their movements carefully. It knew they were planning something.

**The Final Push**

"On my signal," Elias whispered, edging closer to the ravine.

The figure lunged again, its tendrils striking out like lightning. Elias ducked and rolled to the side, narrowly avoiding the dark energy. Liora raised her staff and sent another blast of light toward the figure, forcing it to stagger backward.

"Now!" Elias shouted, charging toward the shadow with all his strength. He swung his sword in a wide arc, cutting through the tendrils that tried to ensnare him. The figure screeched, retreating slightly as Elias pressed the attack.

# THE STORM OF SHADOWS

Liora joined him, her staff glowing brilliantly as she unleashed wave after wave of light, each one driving the shadow closer to the edge of the ravine. The ground beneath them shook as the figure's form flickered, its dark energy struggling to hold itself together.

"We're almost there!" Elias shouted, his heart pounding. "Just a little more!"

But the figure was not done yet. With a deafening roar, it lashed out, its tendrils wrapping around Elias's arm and pulling him toward its core. Elias grunted in pain, the dark energy burning his skin as it tightened its grip.

"Elias!" Liora screamed, rushing forward. She raised her staff, preparing to strike again, but the shadow shifted, its tendrils reaching out to grab her as well.

For a split second, Elias locked eyes with Liora. There was no time to think, only to act.

"Do it!" Elias yelled; his voice hoarse. "Now!"

Liora hesitated, her face filled with anguish, but she knew there was no other way. With a fierce cry, she thrust her staff forward, unleashing the full power of her magic. The light exploded outward, blinding in its intensity, and the shadowy figure let out a screech of fury.

The force of the blast sent Elias flying backward, tumbling toward the edge of the ravine. The shadowy figure, caught in the blast, reeled in agony, its form breaking apart like shattered glass. It staggered, teetering on the edge, before it finally lost its grip and plunged into the abyss.

Elias slid to a stop just inches from the ravine's edge, gasping for breath. He looked up in time to see the shadowy figure's form disintegrate as it fell, its final scream fading into the distance.

Liora rushed to his side, pulling him away from the edge. "Are you okay?"

Elias nodded weakly, his body aching from the strain of the fight. "I think so. Did we... did we get it?"

Liora stood and stared down into the ravine. The shadows had vanished, and the wind had died down, leaving only the quiet sound of the distant river below. "It is gone. For now."

**A Temporary Peace**

As they sat together, catching their breath, the air around them seemed to grow lighter. The oppressive weight of the darkness was gone, and for the first time since the battle began, Elias felt a sense of calm.

But it was short-lived.

Liora's expression remained troubled as she stared out into the distance. "We stopped it here, but that thing... it was only a piece of something much bigger. It was testing us. We barely survived."

Elias clenched his fists. "Then we need to find a way to destroy it completely. Whatever it takes."

Liora nodded, her resolve hardening. "We will. But this is just the beginning. The storm is not over."

As they stood and began their journey toward the mountains once more, Elias could not shake the feeling that the shadow's voice would haunt him for the rest of his life. It had promised to return, and deep down, he knew that when it did, the true storm would be unlike anything they had ever faced.

But for now, there was peace—a fragile, fleeting peace.

And with that, they pressed on, knowing the next battle was already on the horizon.

# Chapter 16

The road to the mountains was long and winding, cutting through a landscape marked by the lingering scars of the storm. The skies remained eerily clear, a stark contrast to the chaos they had just escaped. Yet Elias and Liora moved in silence, their hearts heavy with the knowledge that the calm around them was only temporary.

They had only scratched the surface of the darkness.

"We need to get to the library before the shadows catch up with us again," Liora said, breaking the silence as they crested a hill, the towering peaks of the mountains finally coming into view. The forgotten library, according to legend, held ancient texts, some even older than the world itself. Texts that could hold the key to understanding the force they were fighting.

Elias scanned the horizon, a gnawing feeling still tugging at the back of his mind. He could not shake the image of the shadowy figure plunging into the ravine—its laughter still echoed faintly in his head, as if it were mocking their moment of peace.

"I don't like this quiet," he muttered. "It feels like a trap. Like the shadows are just waiting for us to let our guard down."

Liora nodded, her violet eyes scanning the surroundings as if searching for unseen threats. "That is exactly what they want. But they will not get the chance."

They reached the base of the mountains by nightfall, the temperature dropping as the sun dipped below the horizon. The jagged cliffs loomed above them, casting long shadows that seemed to stretch unnaturally across the landscape. The entrance to the library was hidden somewhere among the cliffs, obscured by years of neglect and overgrowth.

"We should camp here for the night," Liora suggested, eyeing the sheer cliffs with caution. "The climb will be treacherous, especially in the dark."

Elias agreed reluctantly. As much as he wanted to push forward, his body ached from the previous battle, and his mind was weighed down by exhaustion. They found a small clearing near the base of the cliffs and set up camp, the crackling fire offering a small sense of comfort against the encroaching darkness.

## WHISPERS IN THE DARK

Elias sat by the fire, his sword resting beside him as he sharpened the blade methodically. The sound of the whetstone against the metal was soothing, grounding him amidst the tension that lingered in the air.

Liora sat across from him, her gaze distant. She had been quiet since the fight, her thoughts clearly elsewhere.

"What are you thinking about?" Elias asked, breaking the silence.

She hesitated for a moment before speaking. "The shadow we fought back there... it is more than just darkness. It is tied to something ancient. Something that goes beyond our world."

Elias frowned. "What do you mean? Like another realm?"

Liora nodded slowly. "Yes. The Shadow Realm we have encountered is just a reflection, a mirror of sorts. But there are layers beneath it. Realms we do not understand. That creature was a piece of something much older, something that was locked away for a reason."

She paused, her brow furrowing. "I am starting to think the storm was not just random. It was a sign. A warning that something is waking up."

# THE STORM OF SHADOWS

Elias's grip tightened on his sword. "You are saying this is not just about stopping storms or fighting shadows. We are dealing with something far bigger."

Liora's eyes met his, her expression grave. "Yes. And if we do not find answers soon, we will not survive the next wave."

**A Glimpse of the Past**

As the night deepened, the wind picked up, carrying with it faint whispers that seemed to swirl around their campfire. Elias could not shake the feeling that they were being watched—though no shadows moved, the oppressive presence lingered.

"I'll take first watch," Elias offered, his eyes scanning the dark cliffs. Liora, too tired to argue, nodded and lay down, her staff still glowing faintly beside her.

Hours passed in uneasy silence. Elias sat by the fire, his hand never far from his sword. The wind rustled the trees, and the faint sound of running water echoed from somewhere in the distance. But then, just as he began to relax, a soft voice whispered on the breeze.

"Elias..."

He stood up, his sword drawn instantly. His heart raced as he peered into the darkness, searching for the source of the voice.

"Elias..."

It was familiar, hauntingly so. It sounded like—

"Mother?" he breathed, his voice barely above a whisper.

But that could not be possible. His mother had died when he was a child, lost to a mysterious illness that no healer could cure. And yet, the voice was unmistakable.

"Come closer, Elias..."

His feet moved before his mind could catch up, drawn toward the darkness beyond the fire's light. He stepped forward, his heart pounding, the shadows seeming to part before him.

"Elias, it's me..."

He stopped just before the edge of the camp, where the light met the darkness. His hand shook as he gripped his sword, trying to resist the pull of the voice.

Then, from the shadows, a figure emerged.

It was her.

His mother, standing before him, just as he remembered her. Her kind eyes, her warm smile. She looked so real, so alive. Elias felt a lump rise in his throat, his vision blurring with emotion.

"Mother?" he whispered, his voice breaking.

But something was wrong. Her smile was too wide, her eyes too bright. And then, she spoke again, her voice twisting with an unnatural echo.

"Join us, Elias..."

The illusion shattered. The figure of his mother flickered, twisting into a shadowy shape with glowing red eyes—the same creature they had fought before.

"No!" Elias shouted, swinging his sword. But the figure dissolved into mist before his blade could strike.

Liora jolted awake at his cry, her staff glowing brightly as she scrambled to her feet. "What happened?"

Elias stood there, his chest heaving, staring into the shadows where the figure had stood. "It... it was my mother. Or something pretending to be her."

Liora's expression hardened. "The darkness is trying to break you. It knows your weaknesses."

Elias shook his head, trying to steady his breathing. "I almost fell for it."

Liora placed a reassuring hand on his shoulder. "You did not. That is what matters."

Elias nodded, though the weight of the encounter still pressed heavily on his heart. The darkness was learning. It knew how to twist

# THE STORM OF SHADOWS

his fears, how to manipulate his mind. And it would not stop until it broke them.

## The Ascent

Morning came with a bitter chill, but the sunlight did little to ease the tension that hung between them. Elias and Liora packed up their camp in silence, the memory of the night's encounter still fresh in their minds. They had survived another test, but the road ahead felt more dangerous than ever.

The climb up the cliffs was arduous, the rocky path narrows and treacherous. Every step required precision, and the wind that swept down from the peaks threatened to knock them off balance. But they pressed on, driven by the urgency of their quest.

Hours passed, the sun climbing higher in the sky. Just when it seemed like they might never reach the top, Elias spotted something—a faint glimmer of stonework, hidden among the overgrowth.

"There!" he called, pointing ahead.

Liora followed his gaze, her eyes lighting up. "The entrance."

They quickened their pace, their exhaustion forgotten. As they approached, the full scale of the ancient structure came into view. Massive stone doors, carved with intricate symbols, stood before them, partially buried by time but still radiating a sense of power.

"We made it," Elias said, breathless. "The Library of Umbriel."

But as they reached the entrance, a low rumble echoed from deep within the mountain. The ground beneath their feet trembled, and a familiar, cold wind swept through the air.

Liora's face paled. "The storm... it's waking."

And with that, the ancient doors creaked open, revealing the dark, forbidden knowledge within

# Chapter 17

The massive stone doors creaked open, revealing a dark passage that seemed to extend into eternity. Cold air rushed out, carrying with it the scent of ancient dust and forgotten knowledge. Elias and Liora stood at the entrance, their breath hanging in the air as they exchanged a glance, knowing they were about to step into a place that had been untouched for centuries.

"Ready?" Elias asked, gripping his sword a little tighter.

Liora nodded, though her expression remained tense. "Let us not waste time. The storm is coming."

They stepped inside, the heavy doors groaning as they slowly closed behind them, sealing off the outside world. The temperature dropped instantly, the oppressive silence of the library surrounding them. A faint, eerie glow emanated from the walls—runes etched into the stone, pulsing faintly with a long-forgotten magic.

Elias moved cautiously, his eyes scanning the enormous chamber before them. The room stretched on endlessly, rows upon rows of towering shelves filled with crumbling tomes and scrolls. Faded tapestries depicting scenes of great battles and magical rituals hung on the walls, their once vibrant colors now dulled by the passage of time.

"It's... massive," Liora whispered, her voice barely above a breath as she took in the sheer scale of the place.

"This place has been hidden for a reason," Elias said quietly. "The knowledge here... it's dangerous."

Liora nodded, her fingers tracing the glowing runes on the nearest shelf. "We need to find the Book of Shadows. It is said to contain the

## THE STORM OF SHADOWS

history of the Shadow Realm, its weaknesses, and the keys to banishing its power for good."

Elias followed her deeper into the library, their footsteps echoing softly against the stone floor. The silence was unnerving, the weight of the ancient knowledge pressing down on them like a heavy fog.

But as they ventured further, something stirred in the shadows.

**A Watchful Presence**

They were not alone.

Elias felt it first—a faint prickling sensation on the back of his neck, like the feeling of being watched. He stopped in his tracks, his eyes narrowing as he scanned the dark corners of the room. The shadows seemed to shift and move, just out of sight.

"Do you feel that?" he asked, his voice low.

Liora nodded, her grip tightening on her staff. "We're not the only ones here."

A soft whisper echoed through the room, like a distant voice carried on the wind. It was faint at first, but soon it grew louder, more distinct, as if the very walls of the library were speaking to them.

"You shouldn't be here..."

The voice was disembodied, echoing from every direction at once. Elias's pulse quickened, his sword drawn as he turned, searching for the source.

Liora's eyes glowed faintly as she raised her staff, her magic crackling in the air around her. "Show yourself."

For a moment, the library was silent again, the oppressive stillness returning. But then, from the shadows, a figure stepped forward.

It was tall and cloaked in darkness, its face obscured by a hood. Its hands, skeletal and twisted, emerged from the sleeves of its robe. A faint glow emanated from its chest—a pulsing red light, like the eyes of the shadow creatures they had fought.

"I am the Keeper of Umbriel," the figure said, its voice a low, rasping whisper. "This library is my domain. You are trespassers."

Elias took a step forward, his sword raised. "We did not come here to steal anything. We are looking for answers. We need to know how to stop the storm."

The Keeper's hooded head tilted slightly, as if studying them. "The storm is unstoppable. It is the will of the shadows. You cannot fight it."

Liora stepped forward, her staff glowing brightly in her hand. "There is always a way. The Book of Shadows—where is it?"

The Keeper let out a soft, hollow laugh. "The Book of Shadows... a dangerous thing, even for those who seek to destroy the darkness. It holds truths that will break your mind, knowledge that will curse you for eternity."

"We'll take that risk," Elias said, his voice steady. "Where is it?"

The Keeper paused for a long moment, the silence stretching uncomfortably. Then, with a slow, deliberate movement, it pointed toward the far end of the library, where the shelves seemed to disappear into darkness.

"Beyond the Hall of Forgotten Names," it whispered. "But beware. The book is protected. The shadows will not allow you to take it without a price."

With that, the Keeper stepped back into the shadows, disappearing as silently as it had appeared.

**The Hall of Forgotten Names**

Elias and Liora exchanged a glance, their determination hardening. They pressed on, moving deeper into the library until they reached a grand, arching doorway. The inscription above it was worn, but the words were still legible: *The Hall of Forgotten Names.*

"Doesn't sound ominous at all," Elias muttered as they stepped through the doorway.

The room beyond was vast, lined with tall, narrow pillars, each one engraved with countless names in languages neither of them could understand. The air was thick with a sense of loss, as if the weight of forgotten lives hung in the very atmosphere. Soft whispers echoed through the hall, the voices of those whose names had been etched into the pillars long ago.

Liora moved carefully, her eyes scanning the names. "These must be the names of those who once sought knowledge here... and never returned."

Elias's eyes narrowed as he noticed something strange—the shadows in this hall did not behave like the others. They did not simply move with the flickering light. Instead, they clung to the pillars, swirling around the names as if guarding them.

"We need to keep moving," he said, his voice tight.

As they ventured further into the hall, the whispers grew louder, more insistent. And then, without warning, the shadows detached from the pillars, forming into dark, humanoid shapes. Their glowing eyes flickered to life, and the whispers became a cacophony of voices, all speaking at once.

"Turn back... Leave this place... You will join us..."

Elias raised his sword, his heart pounding as the shadowy figures advanced. "Looks like they don't want us getting any closer."

Liora raised her staff, her magic flaring to life as the figures drew nearer. "Then we fight."

## A BATTLE IN THE DARK

The first of the shadow figures lunged, its movements quick and fluid. Elias swung his sword, cutting through the dark mist, but the figure reformed instantly, its glowing eyes burning with malice. Liora blasted another with a wave of light, forcing it to retreat, but more took its place, surrounding them.

"There's too many!" Elias shouted; his back pressed against Liora's as they fought off the advancing shadows.

"We need to push through!" Liora called back, her staff glowing brighter as she prepared a more powerful spell. "They're trying to trap us here."

With a cry, she unleashed a burst of magic, the light exploding outward and sending the shadowy figures scattering. For a moment, the hall was clear.

"Now!" Elias shouted, grabbing her arm as they sprinted toward the far end of the hall.

The shadows hissed and swirled behind them, but they did not stop. At the end of the hall, they found a large, ornate door, carved with symbols that seemed to pulse with dark energy.

"This has to be it," Liora said, panting as she reached out to touch the door.

But before she could open it, the air around them grew cold, and a familiar voice echoed through the hall.

"You shouldn't have come here..."

The Keeper reappeared, its glowing red eyes watching them from the darkness. But this time, it was not alone. The shadow figures began to gather behind it, their eyes glowing brighter, their forms shifting and growing larger.

"You seek the Book of Shadows," the Keeper rasped. "But you do not understand the cost. It will consume you."

Elias stepped forward, his sword gleaming in the dim light. "We don't have a choice."

The Keeper's eyes narrowed. "Then prepare yourselves... for the storm is not the only thing that will destroy you."

With a wave of its hand, the shadow figures lunged once more, and the final battle for the Book of Shadows began.

# Chapter 18

The room erupted into chaos as the shadowy figures lunged toward Elias and Liora. Their glowing eyes gleamed with a mixture of malice and hunger, and their forms twisted unnaturally as they moved with an eerie fluidity, like smoke caught in a violent wind.

Elias was the first to react. His sword sang as he cut through the nearest figure, but the shadows were relentless, reforming in an instant. He gritted his teeth, swinging again, only to be met with the same result. No matter how many times his blade struck, the shadows reformed, their whispers growing louder, more dissonant.

"They're not going to stop," Elias muttered, frustration building. His eyes darted to Liora, who was already summoning her magic, the energy crackling around her fingertips.

Liora's staff pulsed with light as she unleashed another wave of energy. The magic collided with the shadows, forcing them back momentarily, but it was clear that they were regrouping, growing bolder with each passing second.

"They're trying to wear us down," Liora said, her voice strained. "We cannot fight them like this. We need to find the book and get out of here."

Elias nodded, his grip tightening on his sword. "Then we make a path."

Together, they charged toward the ornate door at the end of the hall, pushing through the swarm of shadows that sought to block their way. Liora's magic flared as she sent bolts of light into the darkness, and Elias fought with renewed vigor, his blade slashing through the fog-like forms.

The door loomed ahead, its carvings glowing with an ominous light. The symbols pulsed rhythmically, as if alive and reacting to the presence of the shadows. The Keeper stood before it, a towering figure of darkness, its red eyes locked on them.

"You seek the Book of Shadows," the Keeper said, its voice cold and echoing in the vast hall. "But you do not understand its power. It will cost you more than you can imagine."

Elias did not hesitate. "We'll pay whatever the cost is."

The Keeper's laughter echoed through the chamber, a low, menacing sound. "So be it."

With a wave of its hand, the shadows surged forward once more, but this time, the ground beneath Elias and Liora trembled. The pillars lining the hall began to crack, pieces of stone falling as the entire room seemed to shift. The air grew heavier, charged with dark energy, and the light from Liora's staff flickered as if struggling to stay lit.

Elias glanced at Liora, whose expression was tense, her magic faltering under the oppressive weight of the darkness.

"We need to reach that door," she said, her voice tight with urgency. "If we don't get to the book soon, we won't last much longer."

The Keeper stepped aside, its eyes glowing with malevolent intent. It gestured toward the door, as if inviting them to enter. But Elias knew it was no act of kindness—the Keeper wanted them to open the door, to unleash whatever lay behind it.

"What's the plan?" Elias asked, his voice low.

"We open the door, but we don't let the Keeper control the narrative," Liora replied. "Once we have the book, we get out of here."

Elias nodded, his heart racing. They were out of time. With a final surge of energy, Liora blasted the shadows back, giving them just enough time to reach the door.

**The Forbidden Tome**

# THE STORM OF SHADOWS

Liora placed her hand on the door, her fingers trembling as she felt the dark energy pulsating through it. The carvings glowed brighter, the runes shifting as if alive. With a deep breath, she pushed the door open.

Inside was a small chamber, lit only by the faint glow of more runes carved into the walls. And there, in the center of the room, resting on a stone pedestal, was the *Book of Shadows*.

It was an ancient tome, its cover made of blackened leather, worn, and cracked from centuries of neglect. Strange symbols adorned the surface, shifting and twisting as if they were alive. The air around the book felt heavy, oppressive, as if the very presence of the tome distorted reality.

Elias and Liora stepped inside cautiously, their eyes locked on the book. The shadows outside the chamber seemed to hesitate, as if they, too, were waiting for something.

"This is it," Liora whispered, her voice filled with awe and trepidation. "The book that holds the key to the Shadow Realm."

Elias approached the pedestal, his hand hovering over the tome. He could feel the power radiating from it, a deep, primal energy that tugged at his mind. It was tempting—dangerously so. The book whispered promises of knowledge, power, and control over the darkness.

"Don't touch it yet," Liora warned, her voice tense. "The book is more than just a tool. It is alive, in a way. It can corrupt you if you are not careful."

Elias pulled his hand back, nodding. "So how do we use it?"

Liora stepped forward, her eyes scanning the runes on the pedestal. "We need to unlock its secrets without letting it consume us. The book is said to reveal its knowledge only to those worthies, but it also demands something in return."

"What kind of price are we talking about?"

Liora hesitated, her eyes flickering with uncertainty. "I am not sure. It could be anything. But whatever it is, we will have to face it."

As they stood before the book, the air in the chamber grew colder. The shadows that had been lurking outside the room began to seep in, swirling around the edges of the chamber, watching them. The Keeper reappeared, its eyes glowing with dark amusement.

"The book demands a sacrifice," the Keeper said, its voice low and sinister. "You cannot take its knowledge without paying the price."

Elias clenched his jaw, his mind racing. "What kind of sacrifice?"

The Keeper's eyes gleamed. "A part of your soul. A piece of who you are. The book will take what it needs, and in return, it will grant you the power to fight the shadows."

Liora's face paled, her hands trembling. "No... that is too dangerous. Giving up part of your soul—it could change you forever."

Elias felt the weight of the decision pressing down on him. He could feel the book's power calling to him, offering the answers they needed to stop the storm. But the price... it was almost too much to bear.

"I'll do it," he said, his voice steady.

Liora's eyes widened in shock. "Elias, no. We will find another way."

"There is no other way," Elias replied, his tone firm. "This is our only chance to stop the storm. If I do not do this, more people will die."

Before Liora could protest further, Elias reached out and touched the book.

Instantly, a surge of dark energy coursed through him, his vision blurring as the world around him seemed to warp and twist. The book opened on its own, its pages turning rapidly as ancient symbols glowed with an unnatural light.

Elias gasped, his body tensing as the book began to drain something from him—a part of his very essence. He could feel it slipping away, like a piece of his soul being torn from him. His memories, his emotions, everything that made him who he was, began to fade.

But amidst the pain, the knowledge came.

# THE STORM OF SHADOWS

Visions flashed before his eyes—images of the Shadow Realm, of the ancient beings that ruled it, of the storm that threatened to consume their world. He saw the origins of the darkness, the rituals needed to banish it, and the terrible cost that had been paid by those who tried before.

And then, just as quickly as it had begun, it was over.

Elias staggered back, the book closing with a soft thud. He collapsed to his knees, gasping for breath, his mind reeling from the experience.

Liora rushed to his side, her eyes filled with concern. "Elias, are you okay?"

He nodded weakly, though he felt... different. Something inside him had shifted, a part of him was missing, but in its place was the knowledge they needed.

"I know how to stop the storm," he said, his voice hoarse.

But as he looked up at Liora, he realized that the true battle was only just beginning. The shadows would not let them go easily, and the cost of the knowledge they had gained was far greater than either of them had anticipated.

# Chapter 19

The weight of Elias's words hung heavily in the air. He could feel the shadows lurking, their presence growing stronger as if they sensed the shift in power. The knowledge he had gained from the *Book of Shadows* pulsed inside him, twisting his thoughts, but there was no time to dwell on it now.

Liora's hand gripped his arm, pulling him to his feet. "We have to leave, now," she urged, her voice taut with urgency. "The longer we stay, the more dangerous this becomes."

Elias nodded, still feeling the emptiness within him where the book had taken part of his soul. He could feel the cold seeping in, filling the space with a creeping darkness, but he forced it down. There was no time to fall apart. They had what they needed—now they just had to survive long enough to use it.

Together, they turned toward the door, but the path back was not going to be easy. The Keeper still loomed in the doorway, its red eyes glowing brighter now, as if it had been waiting for this moment. Behind it, the shadows began to gather, their forms shifting and expanding, taking on grotesque shapes.

"You have the knowledge," the Keeper said, its voice echoing ominously. "But knowledge comes with a price. You cannot leave this place without facing the consequences."

Elias stepped forward, his hand resting on the hilt of his sword. His body was weak, but his resolve had hardened. "We are not staying. You will not stop us."

The Keeper's hollow laughter filled the chamber. "I do not need to stop you. The darkness you have taken into yourself will do that for me."

# THE STORM OF SHADOWS

Liora stepped in front of Elias, her staff crackling with energy. "You underestimate us. We have fought your kind before. We will do it again."

The Keeper's form began to shift, growing taller and more menacing. "The storm is inevitable. The shadows are eternal. You may delay the end, but you cannot prevent it."

Elias's mind raced. The storm was still coming, but he now had the knowledge to stop it. Yet, the words of the Keeper gnawed at him—the darkness within him was growing, feeding off the power of the book. Could he really hold on long enough to save them all?

Liora's magic flared brightly as she unleashed a blast toward the Keeper. The room erupted into chaos once more as the shadows surged forward in a tidal wave of darkness, their whispers filling the air with chilling promises of doom.

**The Fight for Survival**

Elias moved instinctively, his sword cutting through the shadows as they swarmed around him. Each strike felt more difficult than the last, the weight of the darkness pressing down on him. The part of his soul that the book had taken—it left him vulnerable in a way he had not anticipated. Every swing of his sword felt like it was draining him, pulling him closer to the edge.

But Liora was there, her magic weaving a protective barrier around them, her determination shining through as she fought off the waves of shadow creatures. Her staff glowed with a brilliant light, pushing the darkness back inch by inch.

"We need to find another way out!" Liora shouted over the din of battle. "The front entrance is blocked!"

Elias nodded, his eyes scanning the room. The shadows were too thick near the entrance, and the Keeper's form had solidified into a towering, monstrous figure. There was no way they could fight through it.

"There!" Elias pointed toward a narrow passage hidden behind a row of crumbling shelves. It was not visible before, but now, in the dim light of their battle, the passage stood out as their only escape route.

Liora nodded, her magic flaring as she cleared a path. "Go, I'll cover you!"

Elias hesitated, but he knew they had no choice. He rushed toward the passage, cutting down the shadows that blocked their way. Liora followed close behind, her magic blasting away anything that came near them.

**The Descent into Darkness**

The passage led them deeper into the ancient library, the walls closing in as they descended further underground. The air grew colder, and the whispers of the shadows seemed to follow them, echoing off the stone walls like a distant wail.

Elias's mind was racing. The knowledge he had taken from the book was swirling inside him, fragments of ancient rituals and arcane spells. He knew how to stop the storm, but it was not going to be easy. The ritual required immense power, and it would come at a cost—one he was not sure he was willing to pay.

"Elias!" Liora's voice cut through his thoughts, pulling him back to the present. She was ahead of him now, her staff lighting the way. "We need to keep moving. The shadows will find us."

He nodded, quickening his pace. But as they descended deeper, he could feel the darkness growing stronger inside him. The whispers were not just in the air—they were in his mind, tugging at his thoughts, trying to bend his will.

*You cannot fight us. The storm will consume you. You will become one of us...*

Elias gritted his teeth, shaking the voices away. "I'm not giving in," he muttered to himself, forcing his feet to keep moving.

The passage finally opened into a large, underground chamber. It was ancient, like the rest of the library, but something about this place

## THE STORM OF SHADOWS

felt different. The air was thick with magic, and the walls were lined with symbols like those in the *Book of Shadows*.

In the center of the chamber stood an altar, carved from dark stone, with an ancient symbol etched into its surface. Elias felt the pull immediately—it was the place where the ritual had to be performed.

"This is it," Liora whispered, her voice filled with awe and dread. "This is where we stop the storm."

Elias approached the altar, his heart pounding in his chest. He could feel the power thrumming beneath the surface, waiting for him to call upon it. But as he stood before the altar, the darkness inside him stirred.

The storm was not the only battle he was fighting.

**The Sacrifice**

Liora joined him at the altar, her hand resting gently on his arm. "Elias, are you sure you can do this? The power you are going to call on—it is dangerous."

"I know," he said, his voice barely above a whisper. "But I must. The storm... it is coming, and it will not stop until it consumes everything."

Liora's eyes were filled with concern. "But what about the price? You have already given up part of your soul. What if this takes even more?"

Elias hesitated, the weight of her words sinking in. He knew she was right—the ritual was not just about stopping the storm. It was about becoming the vessel for the darkness, about channeling the power of the Shadow Realm to banish the storm. And that kind of power always came at a cost.

"I have to try," Elias said, his voice stronger now. "If I don't do this, the storm will destroy everything."

Liora nodded, though her eyes were filled with uncertainty. "I'll be with you," she whispered. "Whatever happens, we'll face it together."

Elias took a deep breath, stepping forward to the altar. His hand hovered over the ancient symbol, the dark energy swirling around him.

The whispers in his mind grew louder, more insistent, but he ignored them. He closed his eyes, focusing on the knowledge he had taken from the book, the ritual that would stop the storm.

With a deep breath, he began the incantation.

The air around them crackled with energy as Elias called upon the power of the Shadow Realm. The symbols on the altar glowed with a dark light, and the chamber trembled as the magic began to take hold.

But as the ritual progressed, Elias felt something shifting inside him. The darkness was not just flowing through him—it was becoming a part of him. He could feel it taking root, seeping into his very being, feeding on the part of his soul that the book had taken.

Liora's voice broke through the haze. "Elias! Something is wrong!"

He opened his eyes, gasping as he realized what was happening. The ritual was not just stopping the storm—it was transforming him. The power of the shadows was too great, too overwhelming.

He tried to pull back, but it was too late. The darkness had already taken hold.

**The Moment of Truth**

Elias fell to his knees, his body trembling as the power surged through him. The storm outside was beginning to calm, but the cost was clear—the darkness was consuming him.

Liora rushed to his side, her hands glowing with magic as she tried to reverse the effects. "Elias, no! You must fight it!"

"I... can't..." Elias gasped; his voice strained. The shadows were everywhere now, filling his vision, clouding his thoughts.

But then, through the haze, he felt Liora's magic. It was warm, like a beacon of light cutting through the darkness. She was pouring everything she had into him, fighting to bring him back.

"I'm not losing you," she whispered, her voice breaking with emotion.

# THE STORM OF SHADOWS

With a final surge of strength, Elias reached for the light, pulling himself back from the edge. The darkness screamed in protest, but he pushed it away, forcing it back into the recesses of his mind.

The storm had been stopped, but the battle inside him had only just begun.

## The Aftermath

The chamber fell silent, the air still and heavy. The storm was gone, its power dissipated. But as Elias and Liora stood in the quiet aftermath, they knew that their victory had come at a great cost.

Elias was no longer the same.

The darkness inside him had been awakened, and though he had fought it back for now, he knew it would not stay silent forever. The shadows were still there, lurking in the corners of his mind, waiting for their chance to take control.

"We stopped the storm," Liora said softly, her eyes filled with concern as she looked at him. "But... what happens now?"

Elias did not have an answer. All he knew was that the real battle had only just begun.

# Chapter 20

The quiet that followed the storm's end was almost unnerving. Outside, the winds had calmed, the clouds had dissipated, and the world was still—but within Elias, a tempest brewed. He could feel it, a gnawing presence at the edge of his consciousness, a dark force waiting to reclaim him. Though they had stopped the storm, Elias knew the shadow would never truly leave.

Liora stood by his side, her face etched with worry. She had not let go of his hand since the ritual had ended, as if her touch alone could anchor him to the light. Her magic had saved him in the chamber, but now that they were back in the world above, they both knew the shadows were not defeated.

"Elias," Liora's voice was soft but steady. "You have been quiet. Are you... okay?"

Elias looked at her, his eyes momentarily unfocused as if he were listening to something only, he could hear. He opened his mouth to speak, but hesitated. How could he explain what was happening inside him? How could he tell her that the power they had used to stop the storm had awakened something far worse?

"I—" Elias started, but the words faltered. "I don't know."

Liora's grip tightened, her magic flaring faintly in response. "We will find a way to fix this. You are strong, Elias. You fought back the shadows before. You can do it again."

But Elias was not sure. The darkness was insidious, not just a force to be fought, but something that felt like it was becoming a part of him. Every step he took felt heavier, every thought tainted with a creeping despair that was not his own. The shadows whispered to him, promising him power, control, and the ability to bend reality to his will.

He pushed the thoughts away, focusing on Liora's voice. She had been the one thing that kept him grounded through all of this. Her light had been the only force strong enough to fight back the shadows. But how much longer could she protect him? How much longer could he resist the pull?

"We need to get back to the city," Elias finally said, his voice low. "There are things we need to prepare for."

Liora's expression darkened. "You're thinking about the Council."

"They're going to want answers," Elias said, his gaze distant. "They will want to know how we stopped the storm and what the price was. But we cannot let them know everything, not yet."

The Council of Mages had always been wary of the *Book of Shadows*. Its power was too dangerous, too uncontrollable. If they knew that Elias had used it—and what it had done to him—they would see him as a threat.

"They don't need to know," Liora agreed. "Not until we understand what is happening to you. We will figure it out together."

**Return to the City**

The journey back to the city was long and fraught with tension. Though the storm had dissipated, the landscape still bore the scars of its passage. Trees were uprooted, rivers had swelled beyond their banks, and the air felt thick with the remnants of dark magic. As they neared the gates, the city guards greeted them with relief, but Elias could feel their unease. They could sense something had changed.

Inside the city walls, the mood was somber. Survivors of the storm milled about, repairing homes, and tending to the injured. The once-bustling streets were now lined with makeshift shelters, and the smell of damp wood and soot lingered in the air. News of the storm's abrupt end had spread quickly, but so had rumors of what had caused it. Some whispered of ancient magic, others of a hidden force that had been unleashed.

As Elias and Liora walked toward the Council's chambers, the weight of their responsibility settled on them. The Council had summoned them immediately upon their return, eager to hear how they had stopped the disaster. But Elias was not ready to share everything. Not yet.

When they reached the grand doors of the chamber, Liora paused, her hand resting on his arm. "Are you sure you're ready for this?"

"I don't have a choice," Elias replied, steeling himself. "They need to know what we are up against. But they do not need to know everything."

The doors creaked open, and they stepped into the room.

**Confrontation with the Council**

The Council's chamber was a vast, imposing room, its high ceilings adorned with ancient banners representing the different factions of magic. At the center sat the six members of the Council, their faces a mixture of concern and suspicion. Grand Mage Valen, the leader of the Council, stood as they entered, his sharp eyes taking in every detail.

"Elias. Liora," Valen's voice echoed through the chamber. "You have done something remarkable. The storm has ceased, and for that, the city owes you a great debt. But tell us—how did you do it?"

Elias took a deep breath, feeling the shadows stir within him. He had to choose his words carefully. "We found the source of the storm," he began. "An ancient power tied to the Shadow Realm. It took... considerable effort to contain it."

Valen's eyes narrowed. "What kind of power? You must be more specific."

Liora stepped in, her voice calm but firm. "It was dark magic. The kind that has not been used in centuries. We had to rely on ancient knowledge to stop it, but the price was high."

# THE STORM OF SHADOWS

Valen's gaze shifted to Elias, and for a moment, it felt as though the Grand Mage could see right through him. "And what exactly was the price?"

Elias met Valen's stare, his heart pounding. "It does not matter now. The storm is over, and the city is safe. But there are... lingering effects. We need time to understand them."

Silence fell over the chamber as the Council exchanged uneasy glances. Valen's expression remained unreadable, but there was a flicker of doubt in his eyes. "Lingering effects? What kind of effects?"

Elias hesitated, the shadows inside him swirling, urging him to speak, to reveal the truth. But he pushed them back. "We need to monitor the city, ensure that the storm does not leave any lasting damage. That is all."

Valen studied him for a long moment before finally nodding. "Very well. But understand this, Elias—if you are hiding something from us, if there is more to this story, it will come to light. And when it does, you will answer for it."

Elias bowed his head slightly, acknowledging the warning. "I understand."

### The Shadows' Call

As they left the Council chambers, Elias felt a growing sense of dread. He had managed to keep the truth hidden for now, but how long could he maintain the lie? The darkness inside him was growing stronger, more insistent. It whispered to him constantly, filling his mind with thoughts that were not his own.

Liora sensed his turmoil. "We need to find a way to stop this," she said quietly. "Before the shadows take over completely."

Elias nodded, but the truth was, he was not sure they could stop it. The power of the *Book of Shadows* was too great, and the part of his soul it had taken was gone forever. He had made a choice to stop the storm, but the cost had been higher than he had ever imagined.

The shadows were rising within him, and Elias knew that it was only a matter of time before they consumed him entirely.

# Chapter 21

The days following their confrontation with the Council were tense and uncertain. Though the storm had passed, an air of dread hung over the city, as if it were merely the calm before a greater tempest. Elias felt the weight of the shadows within him, the darkness gnawing at his sanity, whispering secrets and promises of untold power.

In the quiet moments, he could almost hear the words clearly—sinister, enticing, beckoning him to surrender. But he clung to his memories, especially of Liora and all they had fought for together, using them as a shield against the pull of the dark.

The morning sun barely pierced the dense fog as Elias and Liora made their way to the city's edge, where a crowd had gathered, restless and uncertain. Word had spread that the storm was just the beginning, that a new threat loomed over the horizon. Despite the Council's assurances, the people could feel the shift, the tension in the air that no reassurance could dispel.

Liora leaned in, her voice barely a whisper. "They can feel it too, Elias. They know something is wrong."

Elias nodded; his gaze fixed on the horizon. "The darkness has not left. It is... changed, like it is regrouping. We stopped it once, but it is as if it is gathering strength to strike again."

Liora turned to him, worry etched on her face. "If the darkness returns, you will be the first it reaches. You are still connected to it. What if..." Her voice trailed off, unable to voice the fear they both shared.

Elias closed his eyes, feeling the shadows stir within him. "I do not know, but we cannot wait for it to strike. We need to be prepared this time. And we cannot do it alone."

### The Quest for Allies

Elias and Liora made their way to the city's ancient archives, a place few dared to enter without purpose. The walls were lined with countless scrolls, each detailing past battles, long-forgotten magic, and the old alliances that had once protected the realms. Dust floated through the shafts of light that broke through the high windows, and the air was thick with history and secrets.

"We need allies who know the Shadow Realm better than we do," Elias murmured, scanning the shelves. "There were once mages who studied it, who dedicated their lives to understanding its magic. If any of them survived, they may be able to help us."

Liora scanned the scrolls, her fingers trailing along the spines of ancient books. "I remember hearing stories of the Umbran Order," she said, stopping at a faded tome with a dark symbol on its cover. "They were the only faction who could manipulate shadow magic without being consumed by it."

Elias's eyes lit up. "The Umbran Order," he repeated. "They were exiled, cast out for dabbling in forbidden arts. But they might be our only chance."

Liora opened the tome, revealing pages of illustrations and text detailing the Order's rituals and artifacts. "If any of them survived the purge, they might be hiding in the Wraithwood," she said, tracing a map on one of the pages. "We could find them there."

Elias hesitated. The Wraithwood was a haunted forest known for swallowing traveler's whole, a place steeped in magic and mystery. But if the Umbran Order still existed, they were worth the risk. They were, after all, the last known faction with the knowledge to withstand the shadows.

# THE STORM OF SHADOWS

"We don't have a choice," Elias said, his voice resolute. "If we are to stand any chance against what is coming, we need them. We leave at dawn."

## Into the Wraithwood

The journey to the Wraithwood took two days, each step taking them further from the safety of the city and deeper into unknown dangers. As they neared the forest, the air grew colder, and the landscape changed—trees twisted and warped, their branches reaching out like skeletal fingers. A dense fog blanketed the ground, muffling sounds, and casting everything in a ghostly light.

Liora shivered, pulling her cloak tighter around her shoulders. "This place feels... alive. As if it is watching us."

Elias could feel it too. The shadows within him reacted to the forest's dark energy, as if they recognized it. He was reminded of the *Book of Shadows*, and the whispers that had haunted him since he touched it. The forest felt like an extension of that darkness, a living, breathing entity that pulsed with malevolent intent.

As they ventured deeper, strange shapes loomed in the mist, and Elias could have sworn he saw figures moving in the distance. Shadows shifted and danced, vanishing as quickly as they appeared. The path wound through thick brambles and ancient trees, and the further they went, the more it felt like the forest was closing in around them.

"We should keep moving," Liora said, her voice barely audible in the heavy silence. "If the Umbran Order is here, they'll find us soon enough."

Suddenly, a voice echoed through the trees, low and ominous. "You trespass on sacred ground."

Elias and Liora froze, searching the shadows for the speaker. Figures began to emerge from the fog, cloaked in dark robes with hoods obscuring their faces. They moved silently, their footsteps soundless as they surrounded the pair.

One of them stepped forward, lowering their hood to reveal a stern face with piercing, shadowed eyes. "You seek the Umbran Order," he stated, his voice unwavering. "But do you understand the price?"

Elias took a step forward, meeting the figure's gaze. "We came here because we need your help. The Shadow Realm is stirring, and it is stronger than anything we have faced before. I... I have a connection to it that I do not fully understand. But I need to, or it will consume everything."

The figure's gaze flickered with interest. "The darkness is not something to be fought; it is something to be understood, mastered. But mastery comes with sacrifice."

Elias felt the shadows within him react, resonating with the figure's words. "What kind of sacrifice?"

"Your very soul," the figure replied, his voice like a chill down Elias's spine. "To harness the shadows, one must become one with them. To wield their power, you must relinquish your own."

Liora's hand tightened on Elias's arm. "There must be another way. A way that does not cost him everything."

The figure studied them both, his expression unreadable. "Few can walk the line between light and darkness. But if you are willing, we will show you the path. We will teach you to control the shadows without being consumed by them. But know this—once you begin, there is no turning back."

Elias hesitated, the weight of the decision pressing down on him. He could feel the darkness stirring within him, urging him forward, promising him power. But he knew the risk—if he failed, he would be lost to the shadows forever.

Finally, he nodded. "I'm ready."

## THE RITUAL OF BINDING

## THE STORM OF SHADOWS

The Umbran Order led them deeper into the heart of the Wraithwood, to a clearing illuminated by an unnatural light. At the center of the clearing stood a stone altar, inscribed with ancient symbols that glowed faintly in the darkness.

The leader of the Order gestured for Elias to approach the altar. "The ritual will bind the shadows to you, allowing you to call upon their power. But remember, the shadows are not your allies. They are a force to be controlled, tempered by will and strength alone."

Elias approached the altar, his heart pounding. He could feel the shadows within him pulsing, eager, as if they sensed what was to come. The leader began to chant in a language Elias did not recognize, and the air around them thickened, humming with dark energy.

Liora stood nearby, her eyes fixed on him, her expression a mixture of fear and determination. She had been with him through everything, and he could feel her support even now, grounding him, giving him strength.

As the chanting grew louder, the symbols on the altar flared to life, and a dark, smoky tendril rose from the stone, reaching out toward Elias. It coiled around his arm, cold and suffocating, sinking into his skin. He gasped as he felt it burrow deep within him, fusing with his very soul.

The pain was overwhelming, a searing agony that felt like it was tearing him apart. He could feel the shadows wrapping around his mind, whispering to him, pulling him toward the darkness. But he held on, clinging to the memories of those he loved, the promise he had made to protect them.

Liora's voice cut through the darkness, steady and strong. "Elias, remember who you are. Remember why you are doing this."

With a final surge of will, Elias pushed back against the shadows, forcing them into submission. The darkness writhed, resisting, but he held firm, binding it to his will. Slowly, the pain receded, and the shadows settled within him, quiet and obedient.

The leader of the Order nodded approvingly. "You have taken the first step. But this is only the beginning. The shadows are patient, and they will test you at every turn. Stay vigilant, or they will consume you."

Elias looked down at his hands, feeling the dark power coursing through him. He could sense the shadows waiting, lurking in the depths of his mind. But for now, they were his to control.

As he and Liora prepared to leave the Wraithwood, he knew that the true battle had only just begun. The darkness within him was silent, but he knew it would not stay that way for long. The storm was coming, and this time, he would be ready.

# Chapter 22

The journey back to the city was silent, both Elias and Liora consumed by the gravity of what had just occurred. The Wraithwood seemed to watch them go, as if amused by their new burden. Though Elias had succeeded in binding the shadows to his will, the experience had left a mark on him—one that ran deeper than either of them dared to acknowledge.

The shadows were no longer just a presence inside him; they felt like an extension of himself, a part of his soul that would never let him go.

As they left the twisted forest behind and the city's familiar walls came into view, Elias felt a strange sense of dread. He had gained power beyond his imagination, yet the darkness inside him pulsed with a restlessness he could not shake. The shadows were quiet, yes, but it was a silence that promised much more to come.

Liora looked at him, her gaze concerned but determined. "Elias, are you sure you are ready to face the Council again? They are already suspicious, and after this... there is no telling how they will react."

Elias clenched his fists, feeling the dark energy thrumming through him, responding to his every emotion. "We have no choice. If we are going to face what is coming, they need to understand what we are up against."

**Return to the Council Chambers**

The Council's chamber was quieter than usual, an air of tension hanging thickly over the room. The council members sat in their usual places, though each looked more guarded than before, their faces drawn with worry. Word of the storm's end had spread, but whispers of Elias's new power had spread even faster.

Grand Mage Valen's sharp gaze focused on Elias the moment he entered. "Elias. Liora. We heard you ventured into the Wraithwood."

Elias inclined his head. "We needed answers—ones the city's archives could not provide. We found the Umbran Order. They taught me how to control the darkness within me."

The council exchanged uneasy glances, and Valen's expression hardened. "And now you think you can control the shadows?" His voice held a note of skepticism, as if daring Elias to prove him wrong. "Do you realize what kind of risk you've taken by binding such a power to yourself?"

Liora stepped forward, her tone firm. "Elias took this step because we had no other option. The Shadow Realm's magic is growing, and without understanding its nature, we are vulnerable. He has done what none of us could—to protect this city."

Valen's gaze shifted between the two of them, his eyes narrowing. "Protecting the city does not mean risking everything we stand for. The shadows are volatile, unpredictable. If Elias cannot contain them, he will be more of a threat to us than any storm."

The tension in the room mounted, each word weighing heavier than the last. Elias could feel the shadows within him stir, as if eager to rise to Valen's challenge. He took a deep breath, forcing the darkness down, keeping his voice steady.

"You don't understand," Elias said. "The shadows are not just a threat to me. They are part of a larger force that is gaining strength, one that will consume us all if we are not prepared. I bound the shadows to myself so I could understand them, learn their weaknesses. And I can feel it—the storm was only a prelude. Something much worse is coming."

Valen's eyes flickered with doubt. For a moment, the other Council members exchanged uncertain glances, clearly unsettled. But Valen's

# THE STORM OF SHADOWS

voice remained steady. "So, you expect us to trust you? To believe you can control this power without it consuming you?"

Elias looked directly at Valen; his gaze unyielding. "If I fail, I will pay the price. But I will not stand by and let this city fall."

A tense silence filled the chamber, broken only by the rustling of robes as Valen finally spoke. "Then you'll prove it."

## The Test of Shadows

The council led Elias and Liora to a hidden chamber deep within the Council's sanctum, a place few had seen. The room was carved from dark stone, and the air was thick with ancient magic. Symbols lined the walls, glowing faintly in the dim light, casting an eerie glow over everything. At the center of the room stood a large mirror, its surface rippling like water.

Valen gestured to the mirror. "This is the Mirror of Veils. It was created to reveal the true nature of anyone who looks within. If you can face the shadows inside without being overtaken, we will know your strength. But if you fail..."

Elias knew the risk all too well. The Mirror of Veils was infamous for revealing not only a person's secrets but also their deepest fears, bringing them to life in a way that was nearly impossible to resist. If he investigated it, he would face the full force of the darkness inside him.

Liora reached for his hand, her grip steady. "You do not have to do this, Elias. They cannot judge you based on this test alone."

Elias met her gaze, grateful for her unwavering support. But he knew he had no choice. "If I do not do this, they will never trust me. This is the only way."

Valen stepped back, his expression unreadable. "Whenever you're ready."

Taking a deep breath, Elias stepped forward, staring into the mirror's shimmering surface. As he did, the room faded away, replaced by a dark landscape stretching into eternity. He was no longer in the council's chamber but somewhere else, a twisted version of reality that felt both familiar and foreign.

Dark shapes moved in the shadows, whispers echoing all around him, voices taunting, urging him to surrender. But at the center of it all, a figure stood—his own reflection, yet twisted and darkened, eyes glowing with an unnatural light.

"Is this who you want to be?" the reflection taunted, its voice a mocking echo. "You think you can control me? I am every fear, every doubt you have buried, and I will consume you."

Elias clenched his fists, refusing to let the fear overtake him. "You're a part of me, but you don't own me."

The figure laughed, a hollow, echoing sound that seemed to reverberate through his soul. "Oh, but I do, Elias. You are bound to me now, and the more you fight, the stronger I grow. Why not surrender? Embrace the power, the freedom."

Images flashed through his mind—moments of doubt, anger, the temptation to let go, to embrace the shadows fully. But amid the darkness, he saw memories of Liora, of his promise to protect her and the city, of the sacrifices he had made to get here.

"I won't give in," he whispered, his voice steady. "I've come too far to lose now."

The reflection's face twisted in rage, its form rippling as if it were made of smoke. The whispers grew louder, an assault on his senses, but Elias stood firm, drawing on every ounce of strength he had. With a final surge of will, he reached out, touching the reflection's chest, and forced it back, pushing the shadows away.

The darkness shattered, the whispers faded, and the twisted landscape dissolved. Elias blinked, finding himself once more in the Council's chamber, standing before the Mirror of Veils.

Valen's expression was one of grudging respect. "You resisted."

Elias exhaled, relief flooding through him. "The shadows are part of me now, but they do not define me."

# THE STORM OF SHADOWS

The other Council members exchanged glances; their previous doubt replaced with cautious acceptance. Even Valen seemed to soften, his gaze meeting Elias's with newfound respect.

"You may have proven yourself," Valen said slowly, "but this is only the beginning. The darkness you carry is powerful, but it is a force that must be constantly tempered. If you ever lose control, we will not hesitate to act."

Elias nodded, understanding the weight of the responsibility he now bore. "I wouldn't expect anything less."

## A NEW ALLIANCE

As they left the chamber, Liora placed a hand on his arm, her gaze warm. "You did it, Elias. You faced the shadows, and you won."

Elias managed a faint smile, though the burden of the darkness remained. "For now. But Valen is right—this is only the beginning. Whatever power the shadows hold, it is only growing stronger."

Liora squeezed his hand. "Then we will face it together. Whatever comes, you are not alone in this."

Elias nodded, grateful for her unwavering loyalty. They had both sacrificed so much, and the journey ahead promised even greater challenges. But with Liora by his side, he knew he could face whatever darkness lay ahead.

As they walked through the corridors of the Council's sanctum, Elias felt a flicker of hope, a spark of light in the depths of his soul. The shadows might be bound to him, but he was determined to control them. And with Liora beside him, he would forge his path through the darkness, no matter the cost.

# Chapter 23

The city was unrecognizable. Where once the streets bustled with life, they now lay silent, covered in an eerie twilight that stretched beyond the coming dawn. The citizens had taken refuge, hiding from the strange darkness that settled over everything like a suffocating veil.

At the heart of it all, Elias and Liora stood in the grand square, where the storm of shadows was brewing, swirling into a dense, chaotic vortex. It was here, the final confrontation—where the full force of the Shadow Realm had crossed into their world.

Elias could feel the weight of the darkness within him, pulsing, eager to join the chaos surrounding them. But he had come too far to succumb to it now. He glanced at Liora, her face determined and steady, and the strength in her gaze gave him the focus he needed to face what lay ahead.

"Are you ready?" Liora asked, her voice unwavering, though he could see the worry in her eyes.

Elias nodded, feeling the shadows within him surge, matching the storm outside. "We end this here. I will not let it take anything more from us."

The swirling storm grew louder, an ominous hum filling the air, as if the darkness itself were alive. Suddenly, a figure stepped out from the vortex, shrouded in black and exuding an aura of pure malice. It was a figure Elias recognized—his reflection, the shadowed version of himself he had seen in the Mirror of Veils.

The Shadow Double smirked, its voice a chilling echo of his own. "You thought you could control us? Fool. The darkness is not something you wield. It wields you."

# THE STORM OF SHADOWS

Elias took a step forward, his voice firm. "Maybe so. But I know who I am now. And I am not afraid of you."

The Shadow Double laughed, a hollow, mocking sound that reverberated through the square. "Is that so? Then let us see if your courage holds when you face the truth of what you are."

With a swift motion, the double unleashed a wave of dark energy, shadows lashing out like claws. Elias raised his hands, channeling his own power, and the shadows within him surged, creating a shield that absorbed the blow. The impact rattled him to his core, the darkness whispering, urging him to let go, to surrender.

But Elias held firm, channeling the shadows with a newfound control. He had faced his fears, he had survived the Mirror, and he would not let the shadows consume him now.

Beside him, Liora was chanting, her hands glowing with light. She cast a spell, sending a blinding beam toward the double, forcing it to step back, hissing as the light touched its form.

The Shadow Double sneered. "Fighting together will not save you. You are only prolonging the inevitable."

Elias took a deep breath, feeling the darkness and light within him reach a delicate balance. "We do not have to defeat you alone. We just must keep you here until dawn."

**The Fight for Light**

As the battle raged, the first hints of dawn began to appear on the horizon, faint rays piercing through the dense fog that shrouded the city. The Shadow Double's form flickered as the light grew stronger, its confidence faltering.

Elias could feel it too—the shadows within him were agitated, fearful of the coming light. He looked at Liora, and a silent understanding passed between them. They had to buy time, hold off the shadows until the dawn broke fully.

The Shadow Double lunged at him, shadows swirling, forming razor-sharp tendrils that lashed out. Elias dodged, blocking what he could, but the darkness was unrelenting, pushing him to the brink. He could feel the shadows within him urging him to let go, to join the darkness, but he resisted, drawing on memories of all he was fighting to protect.

"Liora, focus on the light! The shadows weaken with it," Elias called, pushing the darkness back.

Liora nodded, her hands glowing brighter as she concentrated, summoning a beam of pure light that cut through the darkness. The light struck the Shadow Double, causing it to howl in rage and pain, its form flickering, becoming unstable.

"You think you can banish me with light?" it hissed, voice trembling with fury. "I am part of you, Elias. I will always be there, waiting."

Elias took a steadying breath, a fierce resolve filling him. "Maybe you are right. But I choose what I become."

With a final surge of power, he channeled the darkness within him, but not as a weapon. Instead, he accepted it, letting it settle as a part of him, no longer fighting it. The shadows in him quieted, no longer pulling, no longer resisting.

The Shadow Double screamed, its form twisting as it was forced to confront Elias's choice. And as dawn finally broke over the city, bathing the square in golden light, the double dissipated, its form unraveling into tendrils of smoke and shadow, which the sunlight burned away.

When the last shadow faded, the storm cleared, and the oppressive darkness that had covered the city lifted. For the first time in weeks, sunlight poured over the city, illuminating every street, every corner, and the people began to emerge from their homes, blinking up at the sky in awe and relief.

### A New Beginning

As the dawn fully settled over the city, Elias and Liora stood in the quiet square, the echoes of their battle fading. They were weary, but alive, and a sense of peace washed over them—a calm they had almost forgotten.

Liora looked at Elias, a soft smile on her face. "You did it. You faced the darkness and did not lose yourself."

Elias smiled, feeling a lightness he had not felt in a long time. "I could not have done it without you. You kept me grounded, even when I was close to giving up."

Liora reached for his hand, her gaze steady. "We faced it together. That is what matters."

Elias looked out over the city, watching as people emerged from their homes, tentatively returning to their lives. The shadows were gone, but he knew he would always carry a part of them within him. It was a burden, yes, but also a strength, a reminder of all he had overcome.

"What now?" Liora asked, her eyes full of hope and determination.

Elias took a deep breath, feeling the warmth of the sun on his face. "Now, we rebuild. We help the city heal. And we make sure that whatever darkness comes next, we will be ready."

As they walked away from the square, side by side, Elias knew that his journey with the shadows was far from over. But he no longer feared it. He had found a balance, a path through the darkness, and with Liora by his side, he was ready for whatever lay ahead.

The dawn had come, but it was not the end. It was only the beginning of a new chapter—a future where light and dark coexisted, a future he was finally ready to face.

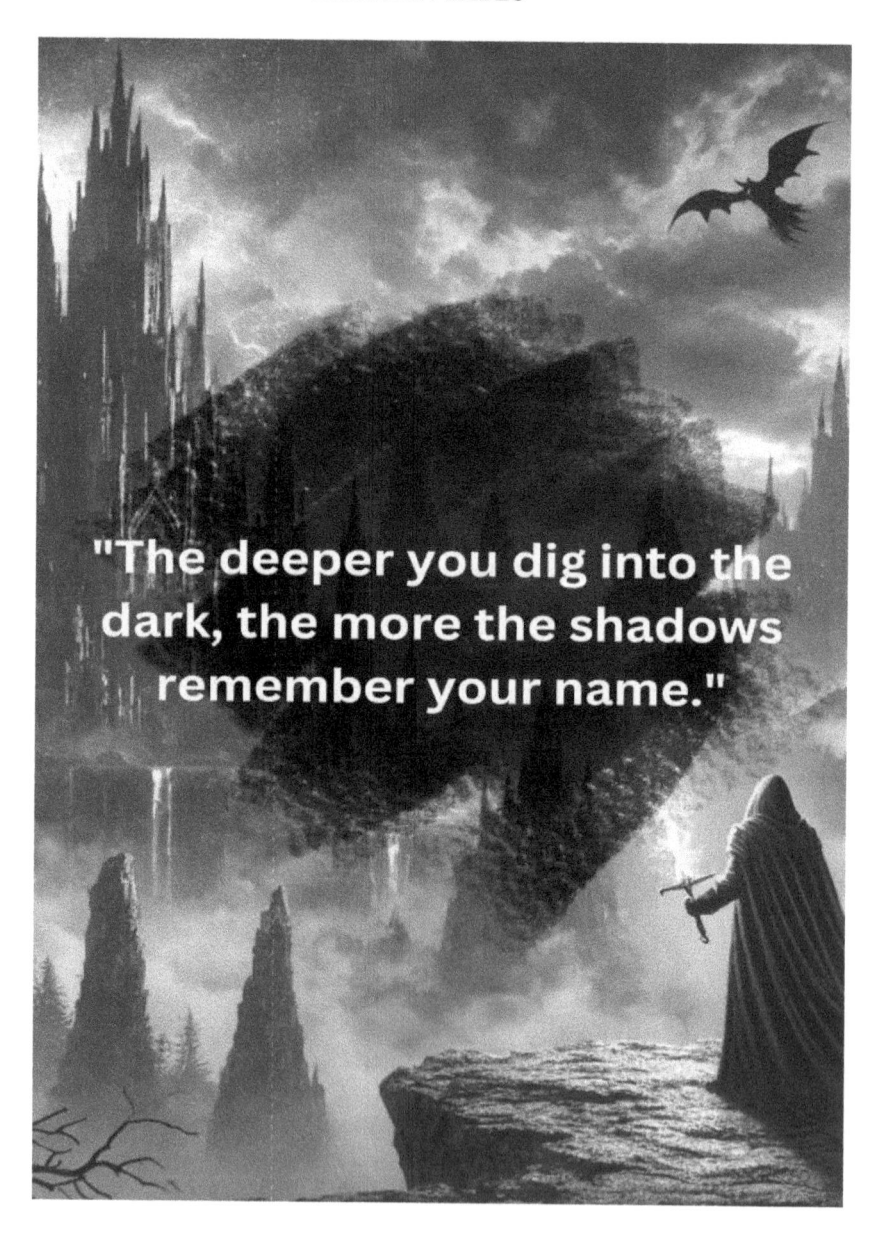

"The deeper you dig into the dark, the more the shadows remember your name."

## Don't miss out!

Visit the website below and you can sign up to receive emails whenever Kirsten Yates publishes a new book. There's no charge and no obligation.

https://books2read.com/r/B-A-WIEEC-FYJIF

BOOKS 2 READ

Connecting independent readers to independent writers.

# Also by Kirsten Yates

**Forget Me Not**
Forget Me Not
Forget Me Not

**The Arcane Academy**
The Weaver's Gambit
The Shattered Veil

**Standalone**
Last summer love
Lily and the bubblegum balloon
The Arcane Academy
Chronicle Of The Lost Arcane
The Storm Of Shadows

Milton Keynes UK
Ingram Content Group UK Ltd.
UKHW020914291124
451807UK00013B/909